"You're a witness...maybe more."

"More what?" she asked.

"You tell me. I'm on your side, Dana. They wanted you badly enough to go after you at home, then on the road, despite the fact that you're being protected. Never assume what they will or won't do."

Dana was more convinced than ever Ranger wasn't playing fair. Then again, nothing about this had been fair—not from the moment she and *Hastiin Sani* had been kidnapped.

"Whatever it is you know, or are keeping secret, is making you a target. Tell me what it is. I can protect you."

Dana shook her head slowly. "I'm not going away."

AIMÉE THURLO

RESTLESS WIND

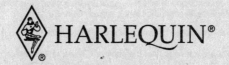

HARLEQUIN®

TORONTO • NEW YORK • LONDON
AMSTERDAM • PARIS • SYDNEY • HAMBURG
STOCKHOLM • ATHENS • TOKYO • MILAN • MADRID
PRAGUE • WARSAW • BUDAPEST • AUCKLAND

To Vivian and Herb, who've kept the fires of their
romance burning for thirty years this month.
Happy wedding anniversary, guys!

ISBN-13: 978-0-373-88785-9
ISBN-10:   0-373-88785-X

RESTLESS WIND

Copyright © 2007 by Aimée and David Thurlo

ABOUT THE AUTHOR

Aimée Thurlo is a nationally known bestselling author. She's published in at least twenty countries worldwide. She has been nominated for a Reviewer's Choice Award and a Career Achievement Award by *Romantic Times BOOKreviews*.

She also co-writes the Ella Clah mainstream mystery series, which debuted with a starred review in *Publishers Weekly* and has been optioned by CBS.

Aimée was born in Havana, Cuba, and lives with her husband of thirty years in Corrales, New Mexico. Her husband, David, was raised on the Navajo Indian Reservation.

Books by Aimée Thurlo

CAST OF CHARACTERS

Dana Seles—Locked within her memory was the deepest secret of the Brotherhood. How could the schoolteacher keep it safe from the warrior who'd captured her heart?

Ranger Blueeyes—He'd fallen in love with the woman he'd sworn to protect, but without her trust, neither of them would survive what was to come.

Hastiin Díil—The new leader of the Brotherhood of Warriors, but what he didn't know could definitely hurt them all.

Ignacio Trujillo—He blamed the Brotherhood for the death of his brother, and the young schoolteacher was an obstacle in his quest for revenge.

Agent Harris—The FBI man chewed up suspects like a pit bull, and Dana Seles was at the top of his list.

Maria Charley—Ranger's former girlfriend had connections that would either lead him to the answers, or just more trouble.

Jonas Sullivan—The trading-post operator was an old friend of the Seles family, but some of his customers belonged to another kind of Family.

Xander Glint—He was in the hospital, charged with kidnapping and murder. Going to prison for life was going to be a lot safer than turning on his boss.

Del Archuleta—He was an ex-P.I. with a ruined reputation and nothing to lose—except maybe his life.

Prologue

Ranger Blueeyes sat with the small gathering of brother warriors inside the cave of secrets, a natural recess in a sandstone cliff high above the tree line of the forest. This site, nearly at the center of the vast Colorado Plateau region of the southwest, had been the Brotherhood of Warriors' gathering place for over a hundred years.

The Brotherhood of Warriors had been established during the time of Kit Carson. Undercover warriors bound by loyalty and traditions, they stood between the tribe and its enemies—an unbroken line of defense. Never seen but always felt, they'd each been hand-selected and tested to the breaking point until only the best of the best remained. The Brotherhood of Warriors existed for one purpose only—so the *Diné,* the Navajo People, could go about their lives in peace and safety.

Tonight, something bad was going down. Ranger could feel the tension in the air. Even the pitch-filled piñon wood fire in the center couldn't push back the chill in the cave. That penetrating cold had more to do with the reason they were here than with the temperature.

Ranger had known the medicine man, *Hastiin Sani,* "Old Man" in Navajo, for many years. *Hastiin Sani* was their leader and also a very gifted crystal gazer, a seer who could foretell the future with uncanny accuracy.

The fact that *Hastiin Dííl,* "Tall Man" in Navajo, was also here tonight told him that his instincts were right on the mark—trouble was heading their way…or had already arrived. Security measures passed down through generations of warriors dictated that their leader and his second were never to be in the same place at the same time unless there was a dire crisis that demanded it.

Hastiin Dííl would be *Hastiin Sani'*s successor someday. There were no secrets kept from *Hastiin Sani'*s second—except one. Only the leader of the Brotherhood of Warriors knew the identities of all the warriors, who also never assembled at the same place and time. In case of an emergency that left *Hastiin Sani* incapable of passing on the names, there was another secure, but lengthier, process in place. In the Brotherhood of Warriors' long history, it had never been necessary to use that alternate method of verification.

Ranger glanced across the way and saw his fraternal twin brother, Hunter, take a seat to the left of *Hastiin Sani*. Hunter now served as HTO, Head of Tactics and Operations.

Hastiin Sani stood and faced those gathered there. "I've seen something deeply disturbing," he began, his voice low and commanding in the nearly total silence inside the cave. "Soon, we'll all be tested…and some of us will fail. Our resources will be taxed to the limit, and our faith in this brotherhood pushed to the breaking point. You're the leaders of our special units so I've called you tonight to prepare you. Although no specific images came to me, just impressions, I can tell you this—the danger I speak of is almost here."

Hunter Blueeyes stood up as the medicine man sat down. "Look, listen, and reach out with your other senses to search for any signs of trouble. I'll be ready to help anyone who encounters a situation. You know how to reach me. I'll be available round the clock until the crisis has passed."

Ranger looked at the light and dark shadows that played on the warriors' faces. He could feel their readiness for action and their desire to fight this new threat.

Hastiin Dííl stood up next. "You're the tribe's protectors—the last line of defense. You've all trained hard and have special skills. Wind, you've been chosen to lead this fight because you excel in unclear situations," he said, looking at Ranger and using his code name only. "Your many lessons at the side of one of our most respected medicine men has heightened your intuitive skills and gives you certain advantages. Prepare yourself, because you'll need to be ready at a moment's notice."

"Just say the word," Ranger answered.

Hastiin Sani brought out four leather pouches, fastened at the top with drawstrings. "These bundles contain medicine from Bears' Ears," he said, referring to a well-known rock formation associated with power and protection. "They'll help protect you against lies, and treachery." He came around the fire to join Ranger, who'd stood to accept the bundle.

"Wind, you bear the name of the guardian of The People. Stay alert. Your beliefs in everything—including yourself—will be challenged."

Ranger nodded somberly. Evil was in the air. He'd sensed that himself at dawn this morning when he'd stood on top of the mesa and listened to the Wind People. Wind carried messages to those who had ears to hear. Wind had warned Youngest Brother of the approach of danger. It would do the same for him.

Once the medicine man left the antechamber, the four remaining warriors nodded to each other then, one by one, left the cave of secrets. No words were exchanged between them. What more was there to say?

Before Ranger could begin the climb down, his brother signaled him. Ranger followed Hunter into one of the smaller caverns.

"I envy you," Hunter said once they were alone. "I miss being out in the field in the middle of the action. Want to flip for this assignment?" Hunter added with a quick half grin, reaching into his pocket.

Before his fingertips touched the coin, Ranger swept his outside leg into Hunter's inside knees, then with a quick hook of the neck, flipped his brother onto the ground. "Tails, I win. Marriage's making you soft," he said with a grin.

Hunter scrambled up, ready to continue the challenge, but *Hastiin Sani* suddenly appeared at the entrance to the side passage. He cleared his throat and, once he had their attention, looked at Hunter. "I need you at council," he said, then disappeared from view.

Hunter grumbled softly, "We should pick this up again sometime." His gaze locked with his brother's. "Be careful, be smart, and if you need me for anything, I'll be there."

"I know."

Ranger left the cave, climbing down the ladder to the piñon-juniper forest below. The threat of imminent danger stirred his restless spirit. Pausing to zip up his jacket, he gazed at the eagle soaring above him against the backdrop of a gathering thundercloud. Using the supporting power of Wind, the fourth guardian of Sun's house, the eagle's flight was unhampered by the violent currents.

Ranger took the eagle fetish he wore around his neck and slipped it inside the medicine pouch. During a mission he always kept the stone carving out of sight in order to safeguard it. Eagle was his spiritual brother. He gazed upward, lost in thought. The eagle, now soaring between the strong up-and-down drafts, had faced his challenge and won. Ranger wondered how he'd fare when his time came. Although he'd been on dangerous missions before, he'd never been pushed to the limits of his skills and endurance.

That would change soon. Many weeks had passed since his brother had led the battle to bring down those who'd stolen a unique antiquity of power, the obsidian dagger, from the *Diné*. Yet, Ranger had sensed that parts of that struggle weren't quite over.

Of course he had no proof—except vague rumors…and the whispers of Wind.

Chapter One

Dana Seles placed her grade book into the top drawer of her teacher's desk, then locked it up for the evening.

Hastiin Sani, as Kevin Cohoe's grandfather was known by the tribe, stood near the door waiting for her. Although she'd been scheduled to meet with Kevin's parents, they'd been called away on an emergency. *Hastiin Sani* had volunteered to attend the conference on their behalf. Things had gone smoothly and they'd discussed arrangements for Kevin to transfer to a more advanced math class.

"It seems like only yesterday *you* were the age of my grandson," he said. "Your mother would always bring you along when she came to my home to visit."

Dana smiled, straightening up her desk, then looking around the room one more time to make sure everything was in order. "I liked going to visit you," she said, remembering how self-conscious she'd been back then. Unlike her, Nancy Seles had been a free spirit who'd thrived on chaos. Nothing had ever been routine at home. "But I hated some of the other places she took me."

"I never approved of her bringing you along to those backroom card games, you know. I told her more than once. But your incredible memory was too much of a temptation, especially when your mom was falling on hard times."

Dana sighed softly. From the day Nancy Seles had discovered that her own daughter had a photographic memory, things had gone totally crazy—and that was saying a lot, since their lives had never been anything even remotely close to normal. "We'd only stay until she'd won enough hands to pay for the rent or groceries, then leave," Dana said, surprised to hear herself defending her mother.

"She wasn't always like that," *Hastiin Sani* said. "She changed after your father's death. She'd depended completely on him and when he wasn't around anymore, she fell apart."

"I was too young when my dad passed away to remember much about him. What I know is mostly from stories I've heard—that he was a good cop, and would never have allowed Mom to raise me the way she did," she said, and shrugged. "But all that's ancient history."

Dana picked up her tote bag, then joined him by

the door. "Are you sure you won't let me give you a ride home? I'd be more than happy to do that."

"No, it's not necessary. A friend drove me here, and another will swing by shortly to pick me up."

Hastiin Sani knew almost everyone on the reservation. Although calling him by his Navajo name, "Old Man," might have seemed disrespectful in some cultures, here on the rez, it was the opposite. She looked at him fondly. He was almost like family. She remembered her mother telling her not to be taken in by his easygoing personality, that *Hastiin Sani* was far more than he appeared to be…. Then again, her mother had never had a firm grip on reality.

Dana locked the door behind them, then walked with *Hastiin Sani* down the hall and out the side door of the building. All the students and most of the teachers were gone now, so the parking lot was nearly empty.

"I wish I could have done more to help you and your mother," he said softly, falling into step beside her.

She stopped and met his gaze. "You did more than you realize. The art patrons you sent us put food on our table more often than not."

He smiled and nodded. "I have *always* been your friend. I'm very proud of you, did you know that?"

Dana stared at her shoes, and cleared her throat. She'd never really known how to take compliments.

"Here's my ride now," he said, pointing with his lips, Navajo style.

She saw the shiny blue pickup pull up just beyond her own white VW bug. A second later, a long-legged, tall and lean Navajo man stepped down off the running board. Some men were made to wear jeans, and the way this man fit into his would have made any sane woman drool. .

His dark eyes fastened on her as he walked toward them with long strides that spoke of confidence and purpose. She nearly sighed as she watched him, but she caught herself in time and quickly pretended to cough.

Hastiin Sani smiled at her. "His Anglo name is Ranger, Ranger Blueeyes. Stay and meet him."

"Er, no, I really should be going." She'd worked hard to have a sane life, one without complications. Though her experience with men was extremely limited, she knew one thing. A man who looked and walked like Ranger Blueeyes was serious trouble.

She and *Hastiin Sani* were walking by an old van when Ranger joined them. He had a smile that could melt hearts, she decided on the spot.

Ranger nodded to her companion, then turned back to her. "Hello," he said.

She smiled and was about to respond when she noticed something out of the corner of her eye. Two men had raised up from the open windows of the van, not six feet away, aiming something in their direction. A heartbeat later she heard two dull thuds, and felt something like a bee stinging her neck.

"Ow!" Dana reached up and pulled out the odd object imbedded in her skin. As she stared at the small dart in confusion, the world started spinning. Her legs were suddenly so weak she could barely stand. Though her vision became blurry, she saw that *Hastiin Sani* had also been hit and had collapsed to his knees. Before she could help him, two men came out from behind the van and grabbed him by the arms.

Kidnappers, she realized. Though disoriented, Dana fought back hard, kicking at the men who were taking her friend. She clawed at the face of the one who had *Hastiin Sani,* and heard him spit out an oath as her nails raked across his cheek. His voice seemed miles and miles away.

Ahead of her she could see Ranger, the man who'd come to pick up *Hastiin Sani.* He was still on his feet and fighting hard, making her wonder if he'd somehow managed to avoid the darts. As she watched, he kicked one man in the chest, bouncing him off the side of the van. Then two more men rushed forward, tackling Ranger to the pavement.

There were just too many…and it was all becoming confusing. Through the fog clouding her brain, she felt someone pulling her roughly into the van, which was open at the side.

In one last desperate attempt to help *Hastiin Sani,* she turned her head and attacked the man holding her. He yelped as she bit him on the forearm. Then someone hit her from behind, and everything faded to black.

DANA WOKE UP lying on her back, with a pounding headache. Her arms hurt, and she slowly realized it was because her hands had been tied behind her back, and she was lying on them. Her mouth felt cottony, and her body ached everywhere.

As her thoughts cleared, she began to remember, and her heart began to pound frantically. She looked around and tried to get her bearings. She was in a small room, but it was almost too dark to see much of anything. The only illumination came from the gap at the bottom of the only door.

She heard faint grunts and thumps coming from the other room. Dana's stomach sank when she realized she was hearing the sound of fists striking flesh. As her eyes got used to the gloom, she discovered she was alone in a small room with wide plank walls and two boarded-up windows. There was no ceiling, just the rafters and a steeply sloped roof. It was probably a mountain cabin, judging from the construction.

Mercifully, the beating taking place in the other room stopped. A minute went by, then she heard *Hastiin Sani*'s voice. His speech was slow and thick, as if the drug from the dart was still in his system. Or perhaps he'd been given something else. The medicine man was reciting names she didn't recognize. After a few minutes, his voice drifted off. Her heart almost stopped as she heard the sound of fists on flesh again but, this time, they stopped quickly. Shortly afterward, *Hastiin Sani* began reciting a litany of names again.

Dana swallowed the bitterness that touched the back of her throat. She knew *Hastiin Sani* was in the other room, but what about his brave friend who'd fought so hard—Ranger Blueeyes? Was he dead? The possibility made her start trembling.

Dana took a deep unsteady breath. She needed a plan. But, first, she needed to free herself. Trying to ignore the way the tough fibers bit into her wrists, she pulled, then relaxed in a persistent cycle as she attempted to create some slack in the rope.

It was tedious, painful work but she gained ground slowly. Suddenly the door burst open. *Hastiin Sani* was thrown into the room and landed hard, facedown, on the floor five feet away from her.

"You finally got smart, medicine man."

The light from the adjacent room gave Dana the chance to make out the features of the man standing between them and freedom. There was no hope of her knocking him out of the way. Their kidnapper was tall and well-muscled.

His gaze was sharp but expressionless as he looked over at her, then back to *Hastiin Sani.* "You were smart to cooperate, old man. You'll live to see the sunrise, and the woman, too. But if the list you gave us is a phony, the school-teacher will pay. Once you get tired of her screams, maybe you'll be more inclined to do as you're told," he said. He looked at Dana again, this time with a leer that left no doubt he'd enjoy carrying that threat through. She tried not to let her fear show, but failed. He laughed, then stepped back and closed the door, locking it behind him.

Dana inched across the floor toward *Hastiin Sani,* uncertain of how she could help him. She was still trying to slip her wrists free of the ropes binding her. Blood from where she'd rubbed her skin raw was running into her palms now. She reached his side then stopped and waited. She called his name softly but he didn't reply.

Then someone in the other room said something about cigarettes. There was the sound of another door closing, then silence. After a quiet two minutes, *Hastiin Sani* rolled over in the other direc-tion and struggled to a sitting position. "I'm glad you're awake," he whispered through swollen lips. "We've got a lot of work to do, and not much time."

Dana could tell that *Hastiin Sani* was doing his best to fight the aftereffects of the drug. Although his speech was thick because of the bruises and cuts around his mouth, his mind was becoming clearer.

"We need to find a way out of here and, to do that, we have to work together," he whispered quickly.

"I've been trying to get loose since I woke up." With one final, painful tug, she managed to slip one hand free. Dana cast aside the rope that had held her hands then went to untie him. As she worked she noticed he was holding a scrap of paper tightly in his fist.

"We need to pry some boards away from that window as quickly and quietly as possible," he said, pointing. "And while we work you'll need to listen to me carefully and remember everything I'm going to tell you."

Together, they began the arduous task of trying to force the boards loose. He pried them with his belt buckle while she used a large nail she'd found on the floor. "These men have no intention of letting me live," he said. "I know too much about their plans and they know I'll do everything in my power to stop them. Your own future is in question as well, particularly now."

"The list of names the man said you gave him… was a fake?"

"No, but I wish it had been. There was no way I could stop myself. All my training, wasted… What I have to do now is destroy the list and hope they won't be able to remember very many names. The man who took the list also dragged me back into this room so I managed to pick his pocket. But the paper tore, and I only got half. I'll have to get the other part that's still in his pocket," he added, shaking his head.

"First, we get out of here. Then we'll find a phone and call the police. They can handle these men," she said in a whisper.

He shook his head. "Listen and remember," he whispered urgently. "A man named Ignacio Trujillo is behind what's happened to us. His name was mentioned in front of me, something they wouldn't have done unless they'd already planned on killing me. We were kidnapped because Trujillo wanted that list of names they forced out of me. He intends to murder those people."

"But what can we do?"

"I belong to a circle of Navajo warriors," he said in a very soft voice. "We exist in the shadows— available on call from our tribal leader to protect the *Diné* when our police and public servants aren't able to do so. No outsider has ever been given the information I'm entrusting to you."

"You belong to a group that works like undercover officers...or spies?"

He paused for a moment. "Not spies, no...more like a proactive defense force. But it's more personal than that and more secretive. Our warriors are hand-selected and trained. Their loyalty to our tribe is without question—their anonymity, absolute. I'm their leader and the only one in the Brotherhood of Warriors who knows the identities of all our members. Those are the names these men wanted."

"But you've got most of the list back, right?" she asked, working to pull out a nail she'd managed to wiggle until it was loose. Seeing him nod, she continued. "Once we get out of here—"

He shook his head. "We can't count on both of us escaping. You're young and unhurt, and less of a danger to them—they think. Your chances are better than mine. This is a time of crisis for the brotherhood and it's crucial that the information on the list reach my second in command as soon as possible. Your photographic memory is the best shot we've got. But first I'll need your word of honor that you'll guard the names on the list from everyone else, including other members of the tribe or even law enforcement officers. The information won't be completely safe with anyone except the one man who has already sworn to protect it with his life. The brotherhood has many enemies."

"You have my word, but it isn't going to be necessary. You'll get out of here, too. We *have* to make it," she said, desperation coloring her words. She pulled the board up and to the side, unblocking a six-inch-wide section of window. Light from the full moon above came in, making their work easier.

"Nothing is certain, but I won't force this on you. I ask only as a favor. The second you memorize this list, you'll be in even greater danger. If you say no, I'll understand."

Dana thought back to her childhood. She would have been a lot lonelier and gone to bed hungry more often than not if it hadn't been for *Hastiin Sani*. "Show me the list."

He handed it to her, and she turned so the light from the moon illuminated the paper. She studied it for fifteen seconds, learning eighteen first and last names. "Okay, I'll remember them," she whispered, handing back the paper.

"The first name on the list is the man you need to find. He's a medicine man and my second in the Brotherhood of Warriors. His Anglo name is Daniel Runningbear, but he goes by the name of *Hastiin Dííl*."

"Got it."

"The list you've seen isn't complete, but it'll do. One last thing. Tell no one what I've asked of you. That'll be your best protection."

"I promise I won't let you down. But we *will* get out of this," she said, renewing her efforts to clear the boards from the window. They now had one board removed, and another was only held in place by one difficult nail at the bottom of the window trim. Two more after that, and they might be able to squeeze through.

He concentrated on his work. "If necessary, I'll do my best to hold them off, but the information you now carry is more important than either of us. Although there's another way for a new leader to learn the names of all the brotherhood members, it takes several days. In that time, our members will be in grave danger and our new leader won't have all the information he needs to defend the brotherhood effectively."

Assured he'd done what was needed, *Hastiin Sani* rummaged in his pocket for matches and set the list on fire, holding it until the last second, then letting it fall to the floor. It burned another few seconds, then he stirred up the ashes with his shoe, making certain nothing remained intact to read. "Now let's hurry and finish up with those boards before the man reaches into his pocket and discovers what happened."

They worked hard, managing to pull another board loose. It looked as if she'd be able to make it out now, and maybe him as well if he maneuvered through sideways. She looked at him, and he nodded, signaling her to go through first. Just then, they both heard footsteps right outside the door.

Hastiin Sani reached through the hole they'd made and pushed open the window that had been boarded up. "Go now!"

"Not without you." Dana reached out to grab his hand but he'd already moved away and headed toward the door.

"Hurry!" he whispered harshly. "Those names *cannot* fall into their hands again. Once they start working you over and pain's all you feel, you'll talk. And no one can blame you. Then they'll kill you. This is your one chance. If you want to live, run! I'll buy you as much time as I can." He jammed a board beneath the door in an attempt to wedge it shut.

The door shook and came open just a few inches. Dana climbed up onto the windowsill, but before she could swing her legs outside, two men burst into the room. Unable to leave her friend, Dana jumped back down to the floor, picked up the closest board and swung it around like a baseball bat, hitting one of the men in the shoulder. The two syringes in his hand flew across the room.

Hastiin Sani kicked the second man in the chest, knocking him back into the edge of the door. As the kidnapper struck the back of his head against the wood, he groaned and staggered back.

Dana knew that they were in a fight for their lives. Their attackers hadn't been carrying dart pistols that time. They'd had those syringes. The men had come back to kill them now that they'd been judged to be of no further use.

She fought hard. Her attacker, anticipating another swing of the board, ducked as he rushed her. But she'd already changed tactics, and this time jabbed him in the gut. He doubled over in pain.

Out of the corner of her eye she saw *Hastiin Sani* kick his attacker's legs out from under him. Then, in a lightning fast move, he jumped on the man, locking his arms around the man's neck.

When her own assailant looked up, pain clouding his eyes, Dana jabbed the end of the board directly into his kneecap.

The man cursed and howled as he fell forward, grabbing his knee. *Hastiin Sani* was on him immediately and delivered a swift blow to the back of the man's head to take out her opponent. But it wasn't over. She could hear other men shouting, moving into the cabin from outside.

Hastiin Sani slammed the connecting door shut and jammed one of the boards under the doorknob. Then he put his shoulder to the door, intending on holding them back with his own strength.

"Go!" he ordered.

"I'll come back with help." Dana jumped up onto

the sill, and swung her legs outside. As gunfire erupted, she looked back and saw the holes that had appeared in the door. Then, to her horror, she saw blood seeping from wounds on *Hastiin Sani's* back. Yet, somehow, he managed to stay on his feet.

"Trust no one," he said, his voice thick with pain.

Dana jumped out, hit the ground, then took one last look back. *Hastiin Sani* was sliding slowly to the floor, blood covering his shirt. But he was still alive. Clinging to that, and knowing she had to bring back help quickly, she raced to the tree line, using the bright moonlight to guide her.

Dana crossed into the forest, knowing her footprints would be hard to track in the dark. She was barely twenty feet into the woods when she heard footsteps directly ahead of her. One of the men must have circled around to intercept her. If he'd come from the cabin, that meant he was extremely fast on his feet—much faster than she was.

Fear invaded every nerve in her body. *Think!* He didn't know where she was, not exactly. It was too dark among the thick vegetation, and he wasn't using a flashlight. She could duck down and hide, remain absolutely still, then wait until he went past.

Holding her breath, she crouched at the base of a thick piñon, and waited. The footsteps seemed to be coming from the direction of the road, not the cabin. Maybe someone had heard the sound of gunfire and was coming up the mountain to help. But the chances of that were slim—false optimism. The kidnappers hadn't been worried about noise, so there probably wasn't another human being around for miles.

The footsteps came closer, and she crouched even lower, searching the ground for something to use as a weapon. There were small, crooked pine branches, but nothing big enough to call a club. That left her with one choice—the large rock near her left shoe. She reached down and grabbed it.

Hitting while holding a rock was better than hitting him with her fist. She looked down at her hand. As far as fists went, hers were pathetic. The closest thing she had to a callus came from holding her grading pencil too tight.

She kept her eyes on the area around her. It was a still, clear night. She heard a soft sound— nothing more than the rustle of a gentle breeze through the leaves. The next instant a big hand clamped over her mouth.

She struggled wildly, trying to hit backward with the hand that held the rock, but her captor clamped his arm around her, pinning her arms to her chest in a viselike grip as he lifted her to her feet.

"Be still. I'm on your side," a rich masculine voice breathed in her ear. "Ranger Blueeyes, remember?"

She instantly became aware of his hard, muscled

chest and strong arms. A second later, he eased his hold. Her heart did a tiny somersault as she turned and gazed up at him. "I thought you were…"

"Dead? Not even close." He had a rifle slung around his shoulder and a knife in the scabbard hooked to his belt. "Now where's *Hastiin Sani?*"

Chapter Two

"He's…" Dana's voice broke, but she swallowed back her tears. "My friend needs help," she managed to say.

There was a flicker of sympathy and other gentle emotions in his eyes, then his expression hardened. "I heard the shots. I'll go get him, but I need to know what I'm up against. How many are there and do they know you've escaped?"

"I saw four men. Two of them were injured in the fight as I escaped. But there may be more."

He nodded, then handed her a set of keys. "My truck's parked about a quarter of a mile down the road. Stay there and lock the doors until the police arrive," he whispered. "I've already called them."

"I don't think you heard me right. My *friend* is back there," she said, anger rippling through her. "I'm not going anywhere. You're armed. Let's go help him."

She noticed the butt of a pistol sticking out of his

pocket. "You've got a rifle, a pistol and a knife. Give me the knife so I can defend myself and I'll show you where he is. We need to get to him before it's too late. He was bleeding badly."

"Your choice," he said, handing her the knife. He looked past her, then brought the rifle to his shoulder. "Get down."

He fired a shot, then motioned for her to follow him. "Hurry, and stay low!" he whispered. "At least two of them are on the move."

They moved quickly to their left. Behind them, there was the sound of bullets striking the tree where they'd been, and nearly simultaneous gunshots from somewhere to their right. They circled as quietly as possible, then stopped behind a rock. The cabin was about fifty yards to their right, and she could see the front fender of the van on the other side of the building. Two more shots rang out, ricocheting off a rock several feet behind them. At least one of the men had moved along with them.

"They're trying to keep us from outflanking them," he whispered. "That knife won't do you much good now. You're going to need my pistol." He pushed something, then handed her the big .45 automatic. "The trigger safety is off. Just point, line up the sights—the post in the middle of the *v*— and squeeze the trigger. But hang on to it tightly with both hands. It's going to kick like a mule.

Once you fire, change positions or they'll zero in on the muzzle flash."

Cold sweat bathed her skin and her stomach was heaving. She sucked in a breath, determined not to give in to the terror she'd kept at bay so far. *Hastiin Sani* needed her, and she'd come through for him just like he'd come through for her so many times in the past.

Dana saw one of the men break from cover and move to their left, running toward the cabin wall. Ranger raised his rifle, but she fired first. As the gun kicked upward in her hand, the trigger of the weapon ripped painfully into the web between her thumb and forefinger. Despite the unexpected stab of pain, she managed to hold on to it. Remembering what Ranger had said, she immediately stepped behind another tree to her left, watching and trying to listen, though her ears were still ringing.

"You forced him back. Good. Just keep behind something solid, and move after you fire," Ranger said, watching the cabin, not her. "Make every shot count, you've got seven more."

"How did you find us?" she asked.

"Friends—and his cell phone," he said, then waited for a moment, watching and listening. "They're not moving. They realize we're both armed now. But they also know we can't get to the cabin without coming out into the open. We'll have to draw them out."

He led her to the right at a brisk pace, choosing a path that led them through some chest-high brush. "They've heard us moving for sure. Now let's give them a target." He reached into his hip pocket and brought out a small flashlight. Then he jammed it into the fork of a sturdy branch and aimed toward the cabin. "Move north to a new firing position as soon as I turn this on."

She looked around her. "North? Are you kidding me? Point!"

He gestured with his chin to their right. "That way. Go!" By the time he clicked the button she was already on the move. Less than five seconds after the light came on, several shots rang out in rapid succession. From her new spot beside a large boulder she could hear branches being clipped and the whine of bullets across the ridge. Suddenly there was a clank, and the light went out. But now they knew the men's positions.

Ranger, several feet to her left, motioned for her to stay low, then took the lead, slipping through the brush and heading northeast. She followed, trying to move as silently as he did, but managed to step on a big branch. It snapped loudly like a fresh carrot. Suddenly several more shots rang out, whining through the trees behind her like angry bees.

Her heart thudding against her ribs, Dana squeezed off two shots in the direction of the gun flashes, then ran forward. The end of the cabin was visible now to her left through the outer ring of trees, and she realized it was long and rectangular, much bigger than she'd thought. The light inside was off, making the structure almost invisible against the forest-covered hillside.

She saw Ranger, up ahead, signal her to stop and get down. On one knee, he brought his rifle up and fired three shots, working the lever quickly between rounds. There was a flurry of return fire, but the shots sounded more distant, and whistled high overhead, not coming even close.

Dana heard the sound of tires rolling across the ground, but then that noise was drowned out by sirens wailing from somewhere behind her, coming up the mountain road. Hopefully, an ambulance had also been dispatched along with the police.

Following Ranger's lead, she moved to the edge of the forest, stopping beside a wide juniper. From there they had an unobstructed view of the cabin. There were four windows on the east side, two on either side of the central door. The window she'd climbed out of was at the far north end, about a hundred feet away. Seeing Ranger advancing, she matched his pace, watching the cabin and praying they'd be able to reach *Hastiin*

Sani in time. He was strong and they'd be able to help him very soon.

"The van's gone," Ranger said. "They must have jumped in and let it roll downhill or we would have heard the engine. I'm going into the cabin. Stay back and behind cover just in case it's a trick."

He'd just finished speaking when they both noticed a thin ribbon of white smoke coming from the window at the far end. A heartbeat later, the entire window blew out, followed by a burst of orange flames.

"He's inside the room at this end! We've got to get him out!" Dana cried out.

Dread chilled her spirit, but knowing that her friend's life depended on them gave her all the energy she needed. "I'm going in to get him."

They heard a vehicle engine start up somewhere well away from the cabin. "The kidnappers are taking off. They heard the sirens, too," he said. "Let's go."

Dana recalled her brief impressions of the room adjoining the one where she and *Hastiin Sani* had been held. "There should be a fire extinguisher on a corner shelf to the right of the woodstove in the main room."

"I'll grab it."

Dana stopped by the first window and called out to *Hastiin Sani,* but there was no response. "I'll climb in here while you go through the front door. Give me a leg up. I left *Hastiin Sani* in this room."

"No, the smoke is already spreading. Let's both use the front door. If we can get to the fire extinguisher, that'll buy us a little more time."

They were at the front door seconds later and found it unlocked. They went inside, through a kitchen to a sparsely furnished family area. There were four wooden chairs, one splattered with blood, and a small round table.

In the bedroom to their left, a mattress burned fiercely, obviously ignited by the scorched kerosene lamp that lay atop what was now a glowing collection of wire springs. A draft was carrying much of the smoke out the window, but enough had drifted into the rest of the cabin to make breathing difficult.

"Go back outside," Ranger said.

"No way," she shot back. "He's in there." She pointed to the splintered door, pock marked with six bullet holes.

Ranger found the fire extinguisher right where she'd said it would be. "We don't have much time," he said, aiming the spray at the flaming mattress. "This won't hold us for long."

While he fought to suppress the fire, she ran into the other room.

Hastiin Sani was on the floor, his lifeless eyes

open, but unseeing. Her heart broke and tears poured down her face as she knelt beside his body. Although deep in her heart she'd known this might be the outcome, she'd wished so hard for a miracle she hadn't been prepared to face this reality.

Hearing Ranger in the room, she looked up and saw him crouched beside one of their captors, the one who'd come after her.

"This one's still breathing," he said.

The words meant nothing to her. Still kneeling by *Hastiin Sani,* and ignoring the blood seeping into her clothes, she gazed at the body of her friend and whispered a soft prayer.

"He held his ground and bought me time to get away. He gave his life for mine," she told Ranger, tears pouring down her face.

She moved her hand over *Hastiin Sani'*s eyelids, shutting them. Then, taking a shuddering breath, she began to cough. "We've got to carry him out of here quickly."

"Our friend's gone. We can't do anything more for him. One of the other kidnappers is also dead. But the man in front of me breathes. He may be able to tell us who was responsible for all this. We'll take him outside first."

The building shook as something crashed to the ground. "Time to move," Ranger said, getting to his feet quickly.

"I'm *not* leaving *Hastiin Sani*'s body here! I'll drag him out myself if I have to," she said, choking back a sob. "I owe him that at least."

"*Don't* speak the name of the dead," he ordered.

His tone captured her attention, jolting her into remembering. Mentioning the name the recently deceased had used in life was said to call his *chindi*—the evil in every man that stayed earthbound after death. Belief in the *chindi* was strong among New Traditionalists and traditionalist Navajos. Even modernists respected the custom.

"I'm sorry," she said, then as she breathed in another lungful of smoke she began coughing again.

"Take shallow breaths and let's work quickly," he said. "I'll carry this man outside. I managed to close the door to the bedroom, so we should still have a clear path. But I'll need you to take the fire extinguisher, just in case. Afterward, if we can, we'll come back for the dead."

Despite the intense sorrow that lay over her like a heavy weight, his logic got through to her. The smoke burned her lungs and her eyes as she led the way with the extinguisher. The door to the bedroom was now on fire, and flames were attacking the door frame and licking at the kitchen ceiling. Soon the whole adjoining wall would go up. The heat was stifling, and the smoke so thick it was like walking through a dimension of Hell. If they'd waited any longer, their way out might have been blocked.

They rushed past the red-hot, burning door, got the unconscious man outside and laid him beneath one of the pines. As Dana looked back, she saw smoke billowing from every window now. Suddenly there was a blast of hot air, and the remaining windows exploded in flames.

Dana took a step forward toward the cabin, searching desperately for a way back in, but Ranger grabbed her, pulled her against him, and held on to her tightly.

"We can't do anything more now. It's time to concentrate on life, not death," he whispered, his voice as compelling as it was gentle.

Almost numb with sorrow, she didn't fight him. Dana buried her head against his strong shoulder, taking the comfort he offered. So much violence and death. Nothing made sense to her anymore… except one thing. Dana remembered her promise to *Hastiin Sani*. It was the only thing she could do for him now, and no matter what it took, she'd keep her word.

The safe haven she found in Ranger's arms tempted her to rely on him, and that's when she stepped away. It was her own strength she'd need to depend on now.

Ranger moved to where the unconscious man

lay and, after searching his pockets, extracted the man's wallet.

Dana, standing behind him, saw that the driver's license listed the kidnapper as Xander Glint. "He's got our friend's cell phone in his shirt pocket," she said, spotting it.

"I'm going to leave it where it is in case someone besides this man handled it. The police might be able to lift some prints later."

For a second she wondered if there'd be any phone numbers saved in it that *Hastiin Sani* wouldn't want anyone to see. But her friend had been too smart for an oversight like that. The only numbers there would be those of friends and neighbors, and maybe a few of the medicine man's patients.

The shrill pitch of the sirens grew louder with every passing second. "They'll be here shortly," Dana said.

"Did the medicine man say anything to you that might explain the kidnapping?"

She said nothing for a moment, wondering exactly how to answer him. Ranger had an eye for details and everything about him said he was a man on a mission. But *Hastiin Sani*'s last words has been *Trust no one,* and she intended on honoring his final wishes.

"Like what?" she asked at long last, unable to think of anything better than answering his question with a question.

"You tell me."

She struggled not to flinch under that gaze. Measuring her words carefully, she finally answered. "He was drugged and beaten up. I got the impression that they wanted to get some information from him. That's all I can tell you."

"Can you remember anything about the men who kidnapped you? Did you hear them say anything that might help us?" Ranger pressured.

Suspicions clouded her mind. She didn't know much about Ranger, but she did know that *someone* had set up and betrayed *Hastiin Sani*. To think that the kidnappers had coincidentally shown up at the right place and the right time, complete with dart guns and knockout drugs, was stretching it. This had been no ordinary kidnapping.

She held back answering. Until she was one hundred percent certain which side he was on, it would be safer not to trust him even with what little she could share.

A police car arrived just a few vehicle lengths ahead of an old fire truck, followed by another police car and an EMT unit. The fire crew went to work right away and a tall, powerfully built Navajo police officer wearing the department's tan uniform came toward them. Ranger nodded, and the officer nodded back. The two appeared to know each other.

While the EMTs worked on the injured man, Ranger gave the officer a quick rundown of what had happened since he'd arrived.

The officer nodded when Ranger finished. "I'll need your weapons," he said, pointing to Ranger's rifle and the pistol still in Dana's hand.

They turned them over to him without question, Dana glad to be rid of the gun.

The officer's gaze shifted to the burning cabin, which had collapsed upon itself and was completely enveloped in flames. "Whatever was in that cabin is long gone. But maybe we'll find a few leads outside." He gestured to the two officers who were circling the burning structure and searching the ground. "It'll take quite a while to process this scene."

The officer looked Dana up and down. "Are you injured, ma'am?"

Dana looked at her torn, bloody clothes, then shook her head. "The blood isn't mine," she managed weakly.

"Your wrists are all scraped up," he said, pointing. "I'll have the EMTs check you over in a moment. Just don't let them near your fingernails. The crime team will want to take scrapings. In the meantime, why don't you two go over and stand by my unit until I can interview you officially? This area is now part of the crime scene."

RANGER AND DANA stood beside the white tribal police SUV, watching the activity. Other officers had now arrived on the scene, and the firemen were hosing down the blackened ruins of the cabin. Two bodies—what was left of them—had been taken by the coroner's people a half hour ago. He was glad he hadn't been asked to help with that. Crime-scene teams and the medical people on the rez used two sets of latex gloves. No one wanted to risk contamination by the *chindi*.

As they watched the police teams work, Ranger gave Dana a long, furtive glance. He had a strong feeling she knew a lot more than she was telling him. He knew she didn't trust him. Of course he didn't much trust her, either. Something about her was…well, wrong. He'd understood her grief and shock. But then she'd done an abrupt turnaround, quickly becoming composed and, along with that, distant and uncommunicative. People had different ways of handling grief, and he thought he'd seen them all. But he couldn't quite get a handle on Dana Seles.

Dana was stunning—even in her conservative schoolteacher slacks and blouse—with curves that could tempt any man with a pulse. She had beautiful copper-colored hair that brushed her shoulders. Her eyes were light brown and soft, doe-like.

Yet when he'd pressed her for information, they'd turned as cold as ice.

The fact that *Hastiin Sani* was dead and they'd barely laid a hand on her raised even more questions in his mind. Why had they bothered to bring her along, unless she'd set up *Hastiin Sani,* then been double-crossed?

Then he remembered how badly the medicine man had been beaten, and what she'd said about him being forced to give up information. Maybe the woman had been brought along as leverage. *Hastiin Sani* would have been almost impossible to break—that is, unless they threatened to torture or violate the woman.

He watched her writing in a little notebook. She'd been doing that off and on for the past twenty minutes. The medics had wanted to bandage her wrists, but she'd settled for a clear salve instead after they'd cleaned them up.

"What's that you're writing?"

"My perceptions about what happened. Not facts...just feelings. Intuitions. Like that," she said, then looked back down and continued writing.

Her handwriting was meticulously neat, as he'd expect from a teacher, but unbelievably small. He couldn't make heads or tails out of it even though he was now sitting beside her on the ground. At long last she stopped, then gazed back at the cabin.

"Think back," Ranger said. "Tell me everything you heard and saw once the drugs wore off."

"I'll be telling the police all of that very shortly. Don't worry," she answered.

"The medicine man who died meant a lot to me and to many other people, too," he said, his voice suddenly hard. "I have to find out *why* this happened. To do that, I'll need firsthand information from you while it's still fresh in your mind. I've got some specialized training, and I intend to get involved in bringing these guys in. You want justice, don't you?"

He watched her carefully. She was being too careful. The way she was weighing every word that came out of her mouth meant she had something to hide. Over the years he'd learned to trust his instincts. Pressing her now was the best way for him to get to the truth—before she had time to put up walls or make up pat answers.

"You told me that you heard the medicine man giving his interrogators some information. Think back. What kind of information?" he asked.

She hesitated. *Hastiin Sani* had died protecting the names on the list. Her best bet at the moment was to try and lie convincingly. "I don't know. I was too groggy and upset at the time, and the door was closed. All I wanted to do was find a way to get us both out of there. I worked on trying to free my hands, which were tied behind my back. I was too scared to think of anything else," she said and shuddered. At least that much was true.

"Think carefully. Is there anything else you can remember?"

"Why should I trust you?" she countered.

He swore under his breath. How was he supposed to explain to this Anglo schoolteacher how much was at stake? "You *know* I was his friend."

"I don't know that at all. All I know about you is that you came to pick him up. And *someone* told his kidnappers where he was. It may not have been you, but I can't be sure of that."

"I helped you get away."

"True, but you appeared out of nowhere—armed to the nines. You shot back at the kidnappers, sure, but, under the circumstances you didn't have much of a choice," she said.

"I had a choice. I didn't have to help you."

She nodded slowly and thoughtfully. "You *did* help me stay alive." She'd tell him enough to make him stop pressuring her. She'd already seen he was friends with the police, so he'd find out sooner or later what she was planning to tell them. "All I know was what the medicine man told me. A person named Ignacio Trujillo is behind the kidnapping and whatever they wanted with us. Trujillo intends to kill a group of people, according to *Hast*...my friend. That's all I can tell you."

"Yes, but is it all you know?" he pressed.

Dana rolled her eyes, but never did answer him. She was telling him enough to keep him off her back, but there was obviously more to the story. Her eyes were alive with secrets.

Out of the corner of his eye Ranger saw a van from one of the local TV stations arriving. Another car raced in right behind the van, one he recognized as belonging to a tribal newspaper reporter.

Knowing the reporters would bring cameras, he walked around to the other side of the police car, hoping to keep a low profile. He didn't want to be spotted and, under no circumstances, could he allow his photo to make the news.

The way Dana followed his lead immediately piqued his interest. It was clear to him that she didn't want to be seen or identified, either.

A dozen more questions popped into his mind. *Who are you, schoolteacher?* His next priority would be finding out everything he could about Dana Seles.

Chapter Three

It seemed to take forever before the two plain-clothes officers, who'd arrived on the scene almost at the same time as the reporters, spotted them. To her surprise, no one seemed curious about why they'd taken steps to avoid being photographed. She knew why *she'd* done it. She didn't want anyone to see her face in tomorrow's newspaper. Yet Ranger's reasons remained a mystery to her. Maybe he was an undercover tribal officer, or member of some other covert agency.

Ranger greeted one of the detectives like they were old friends. "Joe," Ranger said, nodding to him. "What's going on over there now? Have they found anything?"

Joe shrugged. "Not much. Seems the FBI's going to be taking over the case, too. We're just doing the grunt work. You know how it is. You do the work, the feds get the glory."

He nodded. "Any ID on the dead perp?"

The detective shook his head. "His ID melted into a glob, but maybe dental records… Anyway, the bodies are going to be flown to Albuquerque for autopsies and such. Sure glad I'm not going to be there. The fire did a job on them. But we'll get these punks. The medicine man was important to our community."

"Any chance of an ID on the two that got away?" Ranger persisted.

"Maybe. Shell casings were found in addition to those from the forty-five and the carbine. If they have prints, we'll find them," he answered. "Or maybe we'll get lucky and the injured one will have connections that lead us to the rest. Word is he's expected to pull through. With a murder rap hanging over his head, he might give up his buddies."

The detective then turned to look at Dana and gave her a polite nod. "Ma'am." As was customary on the rez, he didn't offer to shake hands. "I'm Detective Joe Nakai."

She gave him her full name and answered his questions. "One of the four men in the van had a small curved scar on the back of his left hand, crescent-shaped. I noticed that before I passed out. They hardly spoke to each other, but I couldn't detect any kind of accent, not even a southeast New Mexico twang."

"After the drug wore off, what happened?"

"When I came to, they were questioning the medicine man, then they tossed him back into the room with me, the one at the north end. That's when my friend told me that a man named Ignacio Ṭrujillo was responsible and would be carrying out even more crimes unless he was stopped. He wanted me to know in case…" Her voice broke and she swallowed. After a moment she added, "In case he didn't make it."

"What kind of crimes?" Detective Nakai asked, looking over at Ranger for a second.

"He wasn't specific but there wasn't enough time." After a pause to clear her throat, Dana continued. "I remember reading in the papers about a man with that same last name. He was the head of a local criminal organization. But he was killed by the police, wasn't he?"

The detective nodded. "You're thinking about Ernesto Trujillo, ma'am. His brother's name is Ignacio." ›

Ranger nodded somberly. He'd had a feeling that they hadn't seen all the ramifications from that case play out yet. Now, Ignacio was after the Brotherhood of Warriors and its members, which, of course, included him. Yet Dana hadn't reacted to his name. If she'd heard *Hastiin Sani* reveal the names of the brotherhood members, his would have been part of the group.

"Would you be able to recognize the ones in the van, or the ones who came after you?" the officer asked Dana.

"I only saw them for a moment, and not under the best circumstances," she said, "but I can describe them, and I can pick them out of a lineup and probably from photos. I have a *very* good memory, detective."

"That's going to help us out a lot, Miss Seles. But the fact that you're an eyewitness makes you a target now," Nakai said, lost in thought.

"They never intended on letting you go, you know that, don't you?" Ranger observed. "From the moment you saw their faces, it was all over."

She said nothing. What more was there to say? She'd come to the same conclusion herself hours ago. Yet the terror she'd felt before had vanished and all she felt now was bone weary. "I know you'll need me to sign a statement and for probably half a million other things, too, but will it be okay if I go home first? I want to take a shower and change clothes." She could smell blood—death—on her clothes. Her head began spinning.

"You're whiter than white," Ranger said, looping his arm around her waist to steady her. "You okay?"

The warmth of his body so close to hers and his strength reminded her of Life with a capital L.

"I'm fine," she said, and moved away. "But how

about it, detective? I'll be glad to put all my clothes in a bag for you, if you'll need them as evidence."

"We will, yes. We'll also need a scraping from under your fingernails before you leave. After that, you can go home and change," he said.

"Can you have someone take me home, then to the police station?" She'd wanted her voice to sound composed, but her last few syllables trembled badly.

"You'll need an escort, of course, considering the situation." The detective looked back at Ranger. "You got another weapon just in case?"

Ranger nodded. "There's another handgun beneath the seat of my truck. My concealed carry permit is current," he added.

"Then go on and escort her to her residence. After the techs take the sample, that is," he said. "The FBI agent will be ready and waiting with his own questions by the time you get to the station. Good luck with him. I know the man, and he's like a pit bull once he gets started. Never lets go."

"Harris?" Ranger asked.

"The one and only," the detective answered.

Ranger blew out his breath in a hiss. "Should have known."

Ranger and the detective exchanged a few more words out of range of her hearing, then Ranger joined her at the crime-scene van.

After the techs had finished with Dana, Ranger went with her back to his truck, his hand beside hers, but not touching. "Officer Nakai's a good man. We got lucky. Otherwise, we would have been ordered directly to the station and you'd have ended up wearing an orange jumpsuit."

That Ranger and Joe had known and respected each other was clear, but there was something else in play here. Maybe the officer expected Ranger to try to question her in a more relaxed setting, and hopefully get more out of her than he had. Information could always be shared. Of course if Ranger was trusted by the police that was certainly a point in his favor. Maybe she didn't have to be quite so cautious around him. But it was too soon to make that judgment…and perhaps trusting every police officer she met might not be a good idea.

"What's on your mind?" Ranger asked quietly.

"I just need a plan…." She hadn't meant to say that out loud, but now it was too late to take back the words.

"A plan? For what?"

For how much to tell him—but she couldn't say that, either. "It goes against everything I am, and everything I've become, to just sit back and wait for others to take care of me. That's never worked well for me in the past, and I have no intention of repeating my own mistakes."

"What exactly are you saying…that you want to go after Trujillo's people?" he asked.

"Not with guns blazing, no, but by taking care of myself and making sure that those who end up going after them have all the information I can provide," she said firmly. And by finding a man who went by the name of *Hastiin Dííl* and giving him the names that were now burned into her memory, she added silently.

"You're holding out on me just as you held out on the detective. I feel it in my gut," he said firmly. "If you know something, now's the time to come clean. The kidnappers that are still free want to stay that way and you're a threat to them. To protect you adequately, we'll need to know what *you* do."

Dana saw the open distrust in his eyes as he gazed at her. He didn't trust her any more than she did him. Considering the stakes, it was the only logical option.

"I don't get it," he said, continuing to press her. "You want the men caught. You've proven that. And you know that's what I want too. But you won't tell me what I need to know. How's that make sense?"

There was something earthy and solid about Ranger that made her want to trust him. He was direct, and honest about what he wanted from her.

"Take me home," she said. Not knowing where

they were, she gave him the address instead of directions.

The drive out of the mountains to the town of Shiprock took about forty minutes. Another fifteen, and they reached her remodeled farmhouse east of Shiprock, just off the Navajo Nation.

As he turned down the gravel road, she gestured ahead. "Second house down, past the apple orchard."

They arrived moments later and she led the way inside, across the covered porch. Realizing he'd have to wait for her, she offered him something to drink. He'd certainly earned some refreshment after what they'd been through. Ranger opted for a cup of her mint tea, and took a seat at the kitchen table.

As she placed the kettle on the stove, she glanced back at him. "I couldn't help but notice your reaction when the detective mentioned the FBI agent's name. Can you tell me more about Harris?"

"You'll see for yourself soon enough. Basically he's a stickler for facts, and he doesn't know when to back off. On the reservation aggression like that's seen as a lack of respect, which guarantees he'll make more enemies than friends."

She nodded slowly. Things *were* different on the reservation. Outsiders often expected the rez to be nothing more than a quaint place steeped in history, or something out of a Hollywood western, but it was far more than that. There were cultural rules of conduct, and transgressions from outsiders were countered with silence and isolation. Word traveled fast on the rez, too. Any outsider who disregarded Navajo ways and stepped on toes would find their reputation often preceded them.

"I answered your question. Now answer one for me," he said. Seeing her nod, he continued. "What's your plan? I know you have one now."

"What makes you so sure?" she asked. She'd never been that easy to read.

"Your attitude. You're no longer distracted or uncertain. You're on a mission. It's written all over you."

Dana took a deep breath then sat down in the chair across from him. "I've seen more violence and death since I stepped out of my classroom today than I have in my entire life. You and I seem to have a mutual friend, and that's why I've already told you what I'll be telling the FBI in a short while. You should be grateful for the courtesy. It's more than you had any right to expect."

"Tell me just one more thing. Why was the medicine man meeting with you at that particular time and day?" he countered smoothly.

It took her a second to process the question. When she did, Dana stared at him in horror. "You think *I'm* working with the kidnappers?" Though on one level she knew that he had no reason to trust her, the implication filled her with a cold rage. "He came to attend a parent/teacher conference regarding his grandson. Kevin's parents were called away on an emergency," she said, her tone as cold as a lake in winter. "Check it out for yourself."

"I will."

His reply just infuriated her more. She wanted to throw something at him but, instead, she went into her bedroom and shut the door resoundingly.

This was the worst day of her life—and it wasn't even midnight yet.

RANGER WATCHED her go. Instinct assured him that her sense of outrage had been as real as they come. But, without facts, he still had nothing. He needed answers—and fast.

One thing continued to nag at him. Her name sounded very familiar to him, but he couldn't pinpoint why.

Irritated, he decided to take a look around her place. He walked into the small den, checking out her desk and the bookshelves, and noted that the room was beyond neat. There weren't any stray papers around, something he'd associate with a middle school teacher, and not even a pen or pencil visible. There wasn't a speck of dust anywhere, either, not even on the windowsill. Considering the wind storms they'd had recently, that was nothing short of a miracle.

He went back into the living room. The school-teacher also liked art. Several oil paintings depicting life on the rez were hung on the walls. As he stepped closer to the largest one over the couch, he saw the signature—Nancy Seles. There was that last name again. He just couldn't put his finger on it…something about a mother-daughter combination…

After a few minutes of looking at the paintings in the narrow hall, he heard her turn on the shower. Moving as silently as Wind, he went to the next doorway and entered her bedroom. The bathroom door across the bedroom was shut, and he heard the sound of a plastic bottle falling in the shower.

Continuing to look around he realized that the woman gave new meaning to the word *orderly*. The clothes in her closet were divided by color, and the four books on the nightstand were alphabetized by author name, not size.

Yet the feel in the parts of the house he'd seen so far was far from austere. The earth-tone colors, the design and placement of furniture and the layout in general combined to give it a comfortable, lived-in look.

Still trying to figure out who she was and why her name seemed so familiar, he went back into the den and sat in front of her desktop computer. It was on, in sleep mode. Familiar with the software, he took a quick look at the files. There were lesson plans, a grade book program with passwords, daily plans, travel plans, and menus for breakfast, dinner and weekends. Dana certainly wasn't big on spontaneity.

He let the computer shift back into sleep mode, then returned to the living room. He was certain he was missing a vital clue. Before he could give it much thought, his cell phone rang. A second later he heard his brother's voice.

"Get me up to speed," Hunter said.

Ranger had no doubt his brother had learned of *Hastiin Sani*'s death within minutes of the police's arrival on the scene. Ranger filled in some of the details for him. "Ignacio Trujillo's out for blood and it's personal."

"Ignacio must have somehow discovered what the medicine man's place was within our brother-hood. Maybe his brother passed that information along to him before we took him down."

"It's also likely Ignacio has plenty of contacts in this area, just like his brother did," Ranger answered.

"What about the Anglo woman? Where does she fit in? Was she just in the wrong place at the wrong time?"

"I don't know yet."

"Women trust you, Wind. Get to the truth. The brotherhood is depending on you."

"I won't let them down."

At that moment Dana came out into the living room. "Let who down?"

"I was just talking to family," Ranger said. She looked completely different. Her wet, copper-colored hair was darker now, still a bit damp, and in those loose-fitting slacks and bare feet she looked smaller…and more vulnerable, somehow. He noticed her toenails were painted a soft pink. That seemed to fit her.

"Are you through with your appraisal?" she demanded with a tiny smile.

He flashed her a grin that had served him well in the past and, judging from her blush, it worked.

"I'll be ready to go in just a few minutes," she mumbled, crossing into the kitchen. "I need to get some shoes, then grab a purse." She took out a glass from the cupboard and poured herself come orange juice from a glass container in the refrigerator. "I need energy," she said. "Want one?"

"Yes, thanks."

She left the carton on the counter. "You know where the glasses are, so help yourself. I'll be back in a minute."

He watched as she walked down the hall, glass in hand, then poured himself half a glass of the juice. The cupboard was as elaborately ordered as the rest of the house, and the refrigerator spotless. After finishing his drink, he placed his glass in the sink. On the wall was a framed sketch done on poster paper with colored markers. It looked like her house, and above it was one word—*haven*.

She came in just then. Seeing him standing there, looking at the sketch, she said, "One of the kids made that for me after I told her that I'd named my home Haven." Seeing the questions on his face, she continued. "I can always relax and find some peace here no matter how crazy my day at school was," she said, then in a somber tone, added, "I didn't know what crazy really was."

Her voice, so vulnerable and so soft, tore through him. He held out his arms, and she stepped into his embrace naturally. It had been a purely instinctive move for both of them.

She settled against him, taking the comfort his compassion gave her. The warmth between them soothed her broken heart and fed her soul.

The temptation to kiss her was almost overwhelming. The way she fit against him awakened something he'd never felt before, something he couldn't quite define…and maybe didn't want to. His grip tightened, and so did hers as she pulled herself closer.

Reluctantly, he released her and stepped back. Too much was at stake to confuse the issue with emotions. If she'd had anything to do with *Hastiin Sani*'s death, he'd see to it that she paid dearly for her betrayal.

"It hurts so much…losing him," she said in an unsteady voice. She took a breath, then added, "I guess we better get going."

As she gathered her things, he watched her. He'd never heard *Hastiin Sani* mention Dana Seles but, then again, *Hastiin Sani* had been the leader of the Brotherhood of Warriors and, as such, his superior. The bond between them hadn't been rooted in friendship as much as brotherhood.

"Okay, I'm ready," she said, picking up the bag with her clothes, then glancing over at him. "How come I looked as if I'd been through a war and you barely look mussed?"

He smiled. "Experience."

Chapter Four

He drove her to the police station at Shiprock, and as soon as they stepped through the entrance doors, a tall, burly man in a dark gray suit hurried across the lobby to meet them.

"About time you got her here, Blueeyes," he growled.

"You're welcome, Agent Harris," Ranger said.

To Dana, Harris seemed like a blur of compressed energy. He looked her over in one quick but thorough glance, then gestured for her to follow him. "There's an empty office down the hall, Ms. Seles," he said. "You and I need a few moments to talk privately."

As she followed the neatly groomed, salt-and-pepper-haired man, she noted the way he paid attention to everything around him. His gaze darted continually from one place to another, and with the rooms all separated by glass panels, he didn't miss much.

Once he sat down behind the desk in an office labeled deputy chief and waved her to an uncomfortable-looking wooden chair, his expression changed. Harris was suddenly focused exclusively on her.

"Ms. Seles, I need you to tell me exactly what happened, beginning from the moment you left your classroom in the afternoon. Include everything you can remember up to the moment the tribal police appeared on the scene."

It took almost an hour. She repeated her story, meticulously describing even the smallest of details. When Dana finished, his expression was one of admiration.

"I don't get many witnesses with your memory," he said. "Not even experienced law enforcement professionals. You certainly don't miss much."

"No, I don't," she answered with complete honesty. "Can you tell me if you've made any progress tracking down the killers yet?"

Harris straightened his turquoise silk tie—the only item of clothing that suggested the Southwest. "There's a four-state manhunt underway for these perps, with patrols on every highway within a hundred miles. Ignacio Trujillo, the name you provided the officers, hasn't been located yet. He's not at any of the properties he owns or controls but we'll find him. The tribal president has already contacted the Bureau demanding justice, which is one of the reasons I'm getting as much extra manpower as I need. Under these circumstances, I have no doubt that we'll catch all the individuals responsible."

"What can I do to help?"

"Right now I need you to look through some photos and see if you can identify any of the perps. If that doesn't work, then I'd like you to work with a sketch artist."

A few minutes later, Dana began searching through a stack of oversized books filled with mug shots. Harris remained across the desk from her as she worked, occasionally taking a phone call, or directing the manhunt. In the background, she could hear several conversations all at once, some in English and some in Navajo, from a half dozen or more officers. She wondered if it was this busy every night.

When she'd searched through all the books he'd given her, she glanced up at him. "The men I saw are not in any of these books. But there's one book missing—number seven."

He checked it out, then muttered a soft curse. "I'll be right back."

When Agent Harris stepped out the door, Dana caught a glimpse of Ranger. He was across the hall speaking to a Navajo plainclothes officer, judging from the badge on his belt. Ranger's expression left no doubt that things weren't going well.

Looking back at the FBI agent, she saw Harris pick up the book she'd been missing off one of the desks. He was on his way back when a stir went around the squad room, and the officers all turned to look at a big-screen TV mounted on the wall. Some stood up from their desks. It became quiet all of a sudden.

Hearing her name mentioned by the newscaster, Dana stood and walked across the hall to listen. Her high school photo was flashed on the screen. The news brief featured her—the kidnap victim who'd survived. As bits and pieces of her life unfolded before the cameras she felt her insides knot up.

"Dana Seles has always been a survivor," the reporter said. "Sources report that in her younger years…"

Dana returned to the office as the reporter recounted her mother's arrest, the charges of card counting and, most of all, references describing Dana's photographic memory.

"This is bad—very bad," Harris said, returning to the office and dropping the book in front of her.

"Because the criminals are going to find out about my photographic memory?"

"Exactly. They might as well have painted a bull's eye on your back," he said, sitting down.

"And whatever details they left out of the broadcast, you can count on reading about in the morning paper."

He leaned back in his seat and regarded her in silence for several moments as she leafed through the mug shots. "Well, at least I know why you were able to come up with that extremely detailed description of what happened today. But there's something I still don't get. Why did you meet with the old man yesterday afternoon?" He looked down at his watch to confirm it was well past midnight. "I understand you were the one who arranged the meeting."

"Teachers usually arrange their parent-teacher conferences," she said, then went through the story again.

"Officers questioned Kevin Cohoe's parents. It seems Mr. Cohoe got a note from someone claiming to be his mother's neighbor and telling him that his mother was very sick. When they got there, Mr. Cohoe's mother was just fine and they realized that the note had been a fake."

"So that's how they knew my friend would be at the school. They set him up." She shook her head, then realized Harris was looking at her very coldly. "Wait a minute. You're not seriously thinking that was *my* doing!"

"You tell me," he said, his expression unchanged.

"Even if I'd been responsible for sending them that note—which I'm not—how could I possibly have known *Hastiin Sani* would show up?"

"A calculated guess? He and his grandson were very close and you two were friends, supposedly."

Rage twisted inside her until her entire body began to shake. "I loved *Hastiin Sani* like a father."

"I'm just trying to sort out the facts," he said in a reasonable tone that only infuriated her more.

"Your theory makes absolutely no sense and *that's* a fact. What motive could I possibly have? I've got a great job, my bills are all paid up and I even have a fairly decent savings account. So why would I do something like that? For more money? *Hastiin Sani's* family isn't wealthy. Last of all, if I were involved, why would I warn you that Trujillo has more violence planned?" Her words tumbled out, along with her frustration and anger.

"Good points. All perfectly logical," he said.

She slammed the mug-shot book shut, then leaned back in her chair and stared at him. "None of the kidnappers are in any of these albums. Now what?"

"We'll need you to work with the sketch artist," he said, his voice cool and impersonal.

As she was led away by another officer, Ranger, who'd been standing in the hall, went in to speak with Agent Harris. She would have given anything to be able to eavesdrop, but she was taken to a different part of the station.

RANGER SAT ACROSS the desk from Agent Harris, his own expression trained into polite neutrality.

"The drug they used on you is common—a generic tranquilizer used by many animal control departments." Harris paused for a moment, cleared his throat, then continued in a methodical and thoughtful voice. "You heard enough of my questioning to know I've got some serious concerns about the motivations of our witness. Correct?"

Ranger nodded.

"I also have some questions about your connection to the medicine man. My gut tells me there's more to it than you've said. Some of the officers around here know what that is, too, but no one's talking." He met Ranger's gaze in an open challenge. "I may not know what's going on yet, but I *will* find out. Why don't you save us both some time and play it straight with me?"

Ranger shrugged. "The medicine man and I knew each other for many years. We were practically neighbors. I was there to give him a ride home after his conference with Ms. Seles."

Harris shook his head. "Don't try to sell me that. There's more to you than meets the eye. You're not just an auto mechanic for some hotshot race car driver." He met Ranger's gaze and held it. A minute stretched out. Finally Harris continued. "But since the right people trust you, you're off the hot seat, for now. Dana Seles, on the other hand, is a real question mark. I don't know if she's been roped into a conspiracy, or was just caught in the middle, but she ties in one way or the other. You having a relationship with her?"

"Hardly. I met her for the first time less than a minute before I took a dart in the neck. The drug wore off in a hurry, and I followed some leads trying to find *Hastiin Sani*. I was about to check out that cabin when I ran into her, or she ran into me."

"I have no evidence that contradicts her story, and she comes across as sincere, but I've got a feeling she's holding back…or maybe she's protecting someone."

He nodded. "I got the same vibes."

"Any chance she may have recognized one of the kidnappers, and had a reason to protect him?" Harris offered.

"She came awful close to shooting one of them in the dark, with no idea which one it was, so I doubt it. What kind of description did she give you of the perps?"

"A lot more detailed than the one the tribal detectives got from you. But they're a match, so she wasn't holding back on that."

"That rules out your protection angle, doesn't it?"

Harris glared at him and didn't answer the question. "Right before you arrived at the station, I received a call from your tribal president. He spoke very highly of you, and suggested that I give you active status on this case." The agent said nothing for a beat, then in a low, conspiratorial voice added, "Talk to me. Are you working undercover for the tribal police, or maybe another branch of law enforcement? Something off the books? I see you've got a concealed carry permit."

"I drive expensive vehicles. You've already checked my background and found I'm an auto mechanic for the Birdsong racing team. Doesn't that answer your question?" Ranger replied.

Realizing that he wasn't going to get more of an answer, Harris shrugged. "Since you've already dealt with Dana, and maybe saved her life, I'd like you to stick with her. You're her bodyguard from this point on—if you're willing. And if she gives you anything that'll advance the investigation, I want to know immediately. Just to be clear, I don't care how important you are to the tribe, I'll still toss your butt in jail if you obstruct this investigation. Am I clear?"

"Pretty much."

Ranger stood up. Let Harris assume whatever he wanted. He didn't work for the FBI. He had his own job to complete.

Almost as if reading his thoughts, Harris rested his fists on the surface of the desk and leaned over. "Listen to me, and listen good, Blueeyes. I don't care who's standing up for you. I'm going to close this case, the faster the better, so don't even think of going cowboy on me. This is no time to make this a tribe-versus-the-FBI fiasco."

"Remember who said that—you, not me, Agent Harris."

"I won't warn you twice." Harris waved to the other officers in the outer room to join them, then in a show of unity, brought everyone up to date on what they had so far, minus the question of Dana's involvement.

"The first twenty-fours of an investigation are crucial. I want everyone on this sharing information and working together. We should have some suspect sketches available soon, so everyone will need copies to distribute."

Seeing Dana coming down the hall, he waved at her to approach. "Ms. Seles, for the time being you'll need to have someone with you around the clock. Ranger Blueeyes served his country with distinction in the military, and he comes highly recommended from the highest tribal authority. He'll be responsible for your security."

Ranger looked at the agent. It was obvious Harris had done a thorough background check on him from the second he'd learned of his involvement. The FBI man was smart and Ranger sensed he'd have to be careful around him.

Dana looked at Harris then at Ranger. "Thanks, but no thanks. A bodyguard will be a disruption in my classroom and will upset the parents. Like all of you, I work for a living and have to teach on Monday. This weekend I'll just be at home grading papers. If you want, you can put an officer outside in my driveway."

Ranger gave her a surprised look. After what she'd been through, he'd expected her to demand one. Her actions only confirmed what he'd already sensed. There was more to Dana Seles than met the eye. His priority would be to uncover what she was so determined to keep a secret.

While Agent Harris briefed and questioned Dana again, now that the artist sketches were finished, Ranger walked outside. He needed time to think. Taking a trail behind the station he climbed atop the mesa that overlooked the northern side of the river valley.

In the silence, Ranger could feel his ties to the land. The reservation was as much a part of him as the blood that coursed through his veins. There, standing in the distance, was Shiprock, a silent sentinel perpetually guarding the moonlit desert below. History's whispers echoed through every canyon and across every mesa. This was the *Diné Tah,* the home of the Navajo. First Man and First Woman had walked here and Monster Slayer had fought the creatures that preyed on the Navajo people. In this sometimes inhospitable land, The People had learned to endure.

Now, they'd need to draw on that strength. Soon, an age-old ritual would unfold. Once news of their leader's death became known, warriors would begin reporting to the secret place, three each day, to make their identities known to *Hastiin Dííl.* The timetable, determined on the day of their induction, had one flaw. Initially, it had been a precaution against enemies who might find them all in one place and kill them. Yet the ancient rule didn't take in to account that, today, people moved more quickly than in the days of the horse-drawn wagon. The brother-hood's enemies could travel hundreds of miles in just a few hours.

In the days ahead, the brotherhood would be more vulnerable than it had been at any other time in recent memory. *Hastiin Dííl* would only be able to deploy the members he knew personally until the process came to an end.

He had to find out quickly what the woman knew. The very survival of the Brotherhood of Warriors could depend on it.

His cell phone rang and he answered it. Ranger recognized his brother's voice immediately. "*Hastiin Dííl* is now our leader and I have your first order. You're to do whatever is necessary to find our medicine man's killers—quickly. If you decide that the woman has critical information, you'll have to push her to get it." There was a pause, then Hunter continued. "What does your gut tell you. Did she set him up?"

"I don't think so, but she's definitely hiding something—from me and from the FBI. Until I know for sure what that is, everything about her is open to question."

"We should discuss tactics. You'll have to pursue leads to Ignacio, even while you're with her."

"I'll push everyone starting with Dana, then follow whatever paths open up. But I need freedom to operate. Don't try to nail me down to plans and strategies. I don't work that way."

There was a tense silence then his brother spoke again. "All right. Your way then. But work fast, Wind."

Ranger placed the phone back in his pocket. Gathering strength from the cool breeze sweeping across the mesa from the north, he climbed back down the path and returned to the station.

She was waiting outside Agent Harris's office when he approached. "Where were you? I gave my car keys to a patrolman, who was going to pick up my car from school and see that it got home. But now that you're my bodyguard, I couldn't leave here until you got back."

"I had something to attend to. Have you been waiting long?"

She shook her head. "No, not really. Agent Harris had a lot more questions. At least he finally knows I'm doing all I can to help him catch those men and that I'm on his side."

Ranger knew the chances of Harris believing that were slim to none, but he didn't argue the point.

"But you've still got questions about me," she said after a thoughtful pause. "I can feel it every time you look at me." She pursed her lips and glared at him. "So why are you sticking around, putting your life on the line for mine?"

"This is what I was asked to do."

"I'm sure the FBI could find an off-duty officer to sit in my driveway and watch the house. All you have to do is say no," she countered.

"The tribe needs me to do this." He could see it on her face. She couldn't quite understand the powerful bond between a Navajo and his tribe. Not that he blamed her for that. From what he'd seen, she had nothing to equate it to.

He didn't know how people without strong cultural roots managed. They were alone in ways a Navajo never could be. Ranger had his family, extended relatives, his clan and linked clans—what Navajos called their "outfit." In Dana's case, since she'd lost both her parents and didn't seem to have any other family around, she was completely on her own.

Ranger set aside his sympathy for her background and concentrated on the issues at hand. Where did her loyalties lie? He still wasn't sure.

As they headed for the station's doors, Ranger glanced over at her. "Did Harris tell you what he intends to do about Trujillo?"

"He said that without physical evidence that actually links Trujillo to the crime all he can do is find him and bring him in for questioning. He'll also be talking to anyone associated with Ignacio, like neighbors, business contacts and such. He plans to put Trujillo under surveillance."

She shook her head and expelled her breath in a hiss. "I thought they'd tap his various phones. But Agent Harris said they'd need a court order and without more evidence, they'd never get one. My information is nothing but hearsay because it was my friend who heard Trujillo's name mentioned, not me. Harris didn't doubt me—it's just not enough to get a warrant or make an arrest."

Ranger nodded. The FBI had a lot of rules to follow. On the rez the Brotherhood of Warriors had more freedom, and was far more effective dealing with problems that often hog-tied official tribal law enforcement.

They were near the door when tribal detective Joe Nakai caught up to them. "I have one last question for you, ma'am. Before the shooting, did the medicine man mention anything to you about any…Navajo business?"

She remembered his name from the list and focused hard to keep her expression neutral. "Just that about Trujillo and his plans for more violence. I think he meant on the reservation, but I can't say for sure."

Detective Nakai nodded, then went back inside the station. Ranger watched him. It was clear to him that Joe had been referring to the Brotherhood of Warriors. Although he'd never seen Joe in their secret chamber, it didn't mean anything. There were many members he'd never met.

"Once you take me back to my place, then what?" she asked, interrupting his thoughts.

"I'll stick close. Think of me as your second shadow."

Chapter Five

"I really don't believe this is necessary—a round-the-clock guard," she said as Ranger's pickup took the wide curve around the Hogback, a large rock formation visible for miles near the eastern borders of the Navajo Nation. Her home was less than ten minutes farther down the four-lane highway. "Those criminals have bigger problems than me right now. Law enforcement officers all over the Four Corners area are looking for them, and have a good idea what they look like. They realize that too, I'm sure, and are on their way to Mexico."

"Not if they're working for Trujillo. They're probably laying low and listening to every piece of news they can get their hands on. Once they hear about your photographic memory, there's no telling what'll happen. You're the only person alive who can make a positive ID," he said in a quiet voice. "You're more of a target now than you've ever been. Even if you have a gun at home for personal defense, you'll have unguarded moments—like when you have to sleep. And you can't take a weapon to school with you."

Accepting those truths was hard and she lapsed into a long silence. The orderly, simple life she'd led up to now was suddenly history. To complicate matters even more, she'd promised her old friend that she'd find *Hastiin Dííl,* but that would be nearly impossible with Ranger breathing down her neck.

She stole a glance at him. Under different circumstances it would have been exciting to have Ranger around—in her house, her car, her life. Ranger was vibrantly sexy and temptingly male. Although she prided herself on being a levelheaded woman who could control her emotions, the tenderness he'd shown her while giving her comfort had awakened a yearning in her for something…more.

Dana shook her head, trying to push those thoughts away. She didn't need this—not now or ever. Love was undependable and never everything it was cut out to be. If you looked to it searching for security, you found yourself standing on quicksand. If you relied on it for companionship, you found yourself alone.

Her mother's life had unraveled after her husband's death. Friends' dreams had shattered as forgotten wedding promises led to bitter divorces. She was better off alone—living in Haven. Her carefully structured life didn't need the kind of distractions—and heartbreak—a man like Ranger would bring.

"Are you okay?" he asked after a long silence.

"No," she answered in a quiet voice. "I *hate* violence. Now I'm stuck in the middle of something I never dreamed could happen—not even in my worst nightmares."

Ranger took his eyes off the road just long enough to reach for her hand. "We met under difficult circumstances, but we're in this together now…to the end. You don't have to feel alone."

His callused palm felt strong and incredibly masculine. Ranger was asking her to lean on him, and heaven knew there was nothing she would have liked more. "You don't trust me, not really. Why are you offering me your friendship?"

"I'm a human being and I know when another human being is hurting," he said, his voice gentle.

She *was* hurting and the warmth of his touch held out the comfort of gentleness—something that was sadly lacking in her life at the moment.

"There's no reason for us not to help each other, is there?" he asked. "The man we knew and lost would have wanted it that way," he said, reminding her of *Hastiin Sani*.

She was ready to yield to his reasoning when reality came crashing down on her, reminding her that caution and survival were inexorably linked. "What are you doing?" she asked, seeing him turn off the headlights as they approached her home.

"If someone's watching your house, we don't want to advertise our arrival."

Despite the fact that everything looked normal, fear pressed in on her until she could hardly take a breath. Death was following her.

She glanced over at Ranger. Although alert, he appeared calm and in control of himself and the situation.

"How can you do this and stay so composed? After all you've seen today, don't you just want to scream?"

"Screaming's not my thing, sweetheart," he said, his eyes suddenly dancing with laughter.

He drove around the flower bed in the center of the circular driveway and parked facing the lane. If they had to leave in a hurry, they'd already be facing in the right direction.

When he stepped in front of her and led the way, Dana fell into step behind him. Outside the rez, a man would step back and let a woman pass first, then catch up and open the door. Navajo customs dictated that the man lead. In case of trouble, he'd be the first to face it.

Dana couldn't help but notice that Ranger seemed ready—almost eager—for a fight. Ranger wanted…maybe needed…action. Pain took many forms.

When he reached the entrance, Ranger suddenly froze. She followed his gaze and, even in the moonlight, could see the dark imprint of a boot just below the door lock. That, and the splintered trim, told them both that the door had been kicked in.

Either from their movement across the old wooden porch, or because of a slight increase in the breeze, the door swung back about an inch. Her heart started to beat so fiercely she could hear it pounding in her head. Through the haze that clouded her mind she felt Ranger grip her forearm.

"Get back in the truck," he whispered.

She was turning around when, from somewhere inside the house, she heard a metallic click.

Ranger pushed her out of the way, then kicked the door just below the knob. It slammed into whomever was standing just on the other side.

There was a groan, then a thud, as the intruder crashed to the floor. A shot went off an instant later, shattering the glass transom just above the door.

Ranger grabbed her hand and they ran to the truck. Dana dove inside the passenger's seat while Ranger took the wheel.

"Stay down!" he said.

She ducked, looking over as Ranger turned the

key and the souped-up engine roared to life. She heard gravel flying as they lurched forward, and took the turn onto the lane faster than she'd ever imagined possible.

Dana bumped her head against the door as she raised up to see how fast they were going. "Slow down!" she yelled. "You'll lose control."

"I *won't* lose control," he said in a surprisingly even tone. "But you're gonna want to fasten your shoulder belt."

As she clicked it in place, she saw a bright flash of light in the passenger-side mirror. "A truck came around from behind my house. Now someone is getting in. They're going to chase us!" Her voice went up an octave.

"They won't catch us, not in *this* truck. Now hang on."

Ranger turned sharply to the right onto the eastbound lane, roared down a hundred yards to a bypass, then made a hard left turn, reversing directions and heading west.

Dana saw their enemies enter the highway, passing in the opposite direction across the median. A few seconds later, the vehicle had made the same maneuver as them, and came up right behind them. "They've got a *huge* truck, loads bigger than this one!"

He glanced in the rearview mirror, at the same

time finally turning on his own headlights. "Six-wheeled pickup. Hot, but it's just a stock model." He reached into his jacket and tossed her his cell phone. "We'll be back on the reservation in five minutes. Press nine. That'll connect you straight to the tribal police. Sergeant Sonny Buck. Tell him what's happened, and give him our location."

She pressed the number. It only rang once before a man answered. "Sergeant Buck."

Dana spoke clearly, but her words came out as fast as her racing pulse. "At least one of the men is armed. He took a shot at us."

"You're on highway sixty-four?"

"Yes, heading west, approaching the curve around Hogback."

"We'll send backup from Shiprock. Can you lose them?"

She relayed the question to Ranger, who was concentrating on his driving.

"I can't outrun them without endangering those people in the slow-moving cars up ahead. That means the punks chasing us are going to close in."

Dana found and pressed the speaker on the phone so that the sergeant could hear Ranger directly and vice versa.

"You've got backup on the way, Ranger. Until then, use your best judgment," the sergeant said.

Ranger focused on the two cars they were

quickly approaching. The cars were side-by-side, taking up both lanes. Judging from the four or five heads sticking out the various car windows and all the waving going on, it looked like two carloads of teens talking back and forth.

He might be able to get around them by passing on the outside shoulder, but to do that and maintain control he'd have to slow down. He flipped on the emergency flashers, hoping to get the attention of the drivers ahead. A girl in one of the cars looked back and waved, laughing.

The driver chasing Dana and Ranger wasn't acting as friendly. As Ranger cut his speed and whipped to the right, the six-wheeler came up on them quickly. Ranger glanced in the rearview mirror and saw a man with a skinhead haircut lean out of the passenger's window, aiming an autoloader handgun.

Ranger weaved more to the right, trying to throw off his aim. "He's trying to shoot out a tire," he said. "Hold on."

As Ranger rotated the steering wheel back to the left, two shots rang out, but both missed the wheels and ricocheted off the pavement, clanging into the bed somewhere near the tailgate.

The gunshots got the attention of the teen drivers immediately. The kids at the windows ducked back inside and the driver on the right braked hard, swerving onto the shoulder. The driver on the left side pulled into the right lane and accelerated immediately.

Ranger whipped the pickup to the left again, speeding past both teen vehicles. "Finally a little more highway."

The six-wheeler was right on their tail, and the heavy vehicle's massive bumper struck their lighter pickup in the right side of the tailgate. Physics took over. Ranger fought to keep them from rolling over as they skidded at an angle down the asphalt. Trying to straighten out their vehicle meant running onto the center median and into the drainage channel. "Hang on!" he shouted.

Dana clung to the arm rest and the seat, staring ahead in horror as they went on the carnival ride from Hell. They bounced hard, nearly running up the other side onto oncoming traffic, before Ranger could steer away without flipping them. He braked hard, and they slid down the center of the shallow trough, throwing up a cloud of dust. Their pickup came to rest just inches from a culvert.

Ranger glanced in the right-side mirror. "They've pulled off to the median behind us, and are getting out of their truck. Get your head down low, like you bumped your head. And stay down. When they get here, I'll handle it."

"But—"

"There's no time to explain," he whispered, slumping down and lolling his head back and against the windowsill on the left, as if he were injured. "Trust me."

Using the side mirror, he saw them coming up the drainage ditch. His left hand was low, on the door latch.

"Stay in the car, no matter what happens next," he whispered, unfastening his seat belt with his thumb and letting it wind up.

He kept the engine running, listening to it. He knew this truck's engine as well as he knew his own heartbeat. It was still growling, low and deep, raring to go.

Biding his time, Ranger watched the pair inch closer. Then the chunkier, muscle-laden weight-lifter-type with the buzz cut picked up his pace, holding the auto-loader casually down by his side. Ranger closed his eyes, feigning unconsciousness, and listened for their approach.

The footsteps stopped, close, and Ranger could hear the man breathing. Putting his entire upper body into the move, Ranger suddenly threw open the door. The metal panel slammed into the weightlifter's stomach. As the man stumbled back, Ranger jumped out and kicked the knee of the second man, the driver. The man screamed in pain and reeled back, but Ranger threw up a roundhouse kick, slamming him in the temple. The man went down hard, out for the count.

Ranger spun to face the beefy guy, who was on his knees among the weeds, searching frantically for his pistol. Suddenly Dana rushed forward, a two-foot piece of split pine, perhaps lost from a load of firewood, in her hand. She swung and cold-cocked the man squarely on the head. He fell forward like a sack of flour.

"Nice hit, but didn't I tell you to stay in the cab?" Ranger demanded.

"I don't always do what I'm told."

Before he could respond, they heard the squeal of brakes from a vehicle close by. "Get in," he said, gesturing toward the pickup. "That might be *their* backup."

They were already in motion as Dana fumbled with her seat belt. They bounced back onto the highway in the oncoming lane, then Ranger did a one-eighty and drove back slowly in the opposite direction. Almost as an afterthought, he rolled his window down and turned on the radio, blaring out a country western tune.

"Why are we going, what, forty-five miles an hour with Brooks and Dunn blowing out the speakers?" she asked, nearly shouting to be heard over the music.

"They'll expect us to hightail it to the rez—my

turf—where I can hide easily. But I'd like to throw them a curveball. If the guys in the six-wheeler are conscious or their backups are still around, they won't take a second look at a slow-moving vehicle coming from the opposite direction."

"Yeah, with the radio blaring." She sat up and shifted into her seat to look at him. "Not a bad tactic. So what's next?"

Ranger gave an approving nod. He liked Dana. Instead of complaining about bruises, or the way things had gone down, she was going with the plan and was ready for the next round. "You have a lot of guts. This is far from what you're used to, but you're catching on fast."

"I learned a long time ago that life has ups and downs, and survival means learning how to bounce back stronger than before."

He'd heard the echo of painful memories that wound through her words, but that was only because he had a habit of really listening to people, and reading between the lines. Dana wasn't asking for his sympathy. She was simply stating a fact.

"I work for Birdsong Enterprises. We're going back to Farmington to switch vehicles," he said, turning the radio off now that they were past the area where the confrontation had taken place. As they'd gone by, he'd noted with satisfaction that the six-wheeler hadn't moved.

"Birdsong…the stock car racing family?" she asked.

He nodded, picking up speed to match the posted limit. "I work in their auto performance shop."

"The Birdsongs will let you just borrow one of their cars?"

"Sure." The Birdsong brothers weren't full Navajo, but the tribe was one of their racing team sponsors. The Brotherhood of Warriors usually bought their modified pickups and cars from the Birdsongs, too. The brothers had learned not to ask questions, especially since the warriors' financial backing came from the tribal president's special fund.

Ranger reached for the cell phone and made a call. "Tony, this is Ranger. Hope I didn't wake you up, buddy, but I need a new set of wheels ASAP. What's available?"

"We've got that new model everyone in law enforcement is salivating for—and we've made some improvements on it, too. It'll run circles around every bad guy on the road. And guess what, The Ringer just came out of the shop an hour ago, and she's ready to roll."

Ranger smiled. He'd driven the generic-looking pale blue sedan. It was disguised to look like something Granny might drive to her quilting group, complete with knitted baby shoes dangling from the rearview mirror. Yet it had a racing and handling setup that could beat most high-performance vehicles. It had started out as a joke, but once everyone at Birdsong had gotten involved, it had ended up being one of the fastest cars around. Everyone wanted a chance to get behind the wheel. The car was hot, and constantly being tweaked to raise the bar a little higher.

"It's gotta be The Ringer. Can you meet me in the parking lot of the Terminal Café—West Side Mall? We'll trade keys. You can take my truck."

"I've always had my eye on that truck of yours. What do you say I keep your little jewel for the weekend?"

Ranger laughed. "Yeah, fine."

"Any other way I can help?"

"No, I've got it covered. Thanks," Ranger answered, keeping it vague.

Switching off the phone, Ranger glanced over at her. "I'm going to borrow one of Tony Birdsong's best kept secrets."

Dana didn't press him for more details. As he headed back to Farmington, Ranger wondered about the woman next to him. What she lacked in training, she more than made up for in spirit. He found himself liking her more by the hour.

Chapter Six

Dana looked at her watch. "It's two a.m.," she said, yawning. "I'm tired, and I'm just not thinking straight anymore. I need some sleep. Can we go back to my place and get a few hours of sleep? I understand criminals don't return to the scene of the crime."

"Who gave you that lesson in crime fighting? Was it in your teacher's manual?" he teased.

"I heard it on TV," she answered, annoyed. "But it makes sense."

"Not in this case. They wanted you badly enough to go after you at home, then on the road, despite the fact that you're being protected. Never assume what the bad guys will or won't do." He glanced over at her. She was tired so her resistance would be low. Now was the ideal time to press her for answers.

"You're a witness…maybe more."

"More than what?" she asked, rubbing her eyes.

"You tell me. I'm on *your* side, Dana. You must

have noticed that by now. Whatever it is you know, or are keeping secret, is making you a target. Tell me what it is. Then I can pull some strings and hide you somewhere, maybe out of state, until these guys are caught."

She shook her head slowly. "I'm not going away. I've got business here."

"Business?"

"Yeah. I'm a teacher in Shiprock." Although she knew he was a good ally, she had a secret she'd vowed to protect. It would probably be better for her not to talk at all right now rather than risk any slipups. "I'm going to lay back for a few minutes. If I fall asleep and you need something, wake me."

"I could use some company, too. Talk to me. I need to stay sharp."

Dana was more convinced than ever that he wasn't playing fair. Then again, nothing about this had been fair—not from the moment she and *Hastiin Sani* had been kidnapped.

"So we'll talk, but don't expect much," she said, yawning.

"Tell me, how did you and our medicine man become friends?"

It appeared to be an innocent question, but she could practically feel the undercurrent there. "You already know how it was for me growing up. Back then, the medicine man was my unofficial guardian angel. He was *always* there for me, no matter what."

"And you remained close friends all these years?"

She nodded. "He was one of my character references when I applied for my teaching job in Shiprock. Lately, he'd become very involved with some tribal consulting work so we hadn't gotten together since the beginning of the school year. I was really happy to see him when he showed up at the parent/teacher conference I'd scheduled with his son and wife." Her voice shook and she lapsed into an uncomfortable silence. "And you?" she finally added.

"I've known him for a very long time. He's the man I'd always look to for answers."

"Then you'll miss him as much as I will," she said with a soft sigh.

His face remained without expression for a moment, then his eyes softened and he nodded solemnly.

Though he hadn't said much, she could feel his grief as clearly as she did her own. A very precious life had been lost. "I wish I were home right now, grading papers, and none of this had ever happened."

"The pain will pass, and the papers will still be there for you when this is over."

She yawned, leaning back, her eyes automatically closing. "It'll end soon. It has to," she murmured, then drifted off to sleep.

Ranger glanced at Dana. She was exhausted and he didn't have the heart to wake her.

DANA WOKE UP when the truck came to a stop. The lights of the parking lot were bright and it was hard to stop squinting and get her eyes to focus.

Ranger placed a hand on her shoulder. "Wait for me here. I'm not going far."

Her senses numbed with exhaustion, she tried to concentrate on the conversation he was having with the other man.

"If you want to stay below the radar for a few days, I'll be glad to pass along a message to your brother," the man she took to be Tony Birdsong said.

"Not necessary. But thanks for bringing the car."

Hearing a bunch of car details that meant absolutely nothing to her, Dana drifted off to sleep again. In a sleepy haze, she felt strong arms lifting her out of the pickup. Without even opening her eyes she knew it was Ranger. He had a special outdoor woodsy scent about him that seemed to fit in perfectly with the man he was. Dana rested her head against his shoulder, comforted by the warmth of his strong, male body.

Awareness and desire ribboned around her—and that suddenly brought her back to a state of alertness. "Put me down, Ranger," she said, her eyes wide open. "I'm perfectly capable of walking."

He laughed. "Enjoy the luxury while you can. You're so tired you can't see straight."

"You've got to be worn out yourself, and if you faint from exhaustion, I'll need a forklift to carry you."

The chuckle started like a low rumble in his chest, then became a full-throated laugh as Ranger set her down.

For a brief second Dana stared at the old car, wondering if Ranger was playing a joke on her. The two-door sedan had its original finish—a medium blue that was nearly gray in places from oxidation.

The interior, from what she could see from her position by the passenger's side, was original, not including the almost matching blue tape that covered several splits in the vinyl dashboard. The upholstery was covered with stretchy terry cloth in a pale green—machine washable, no doubt. A battery-powered radio, one of those probably offered free with a magazine subscription, occupied a portion of the gaping hole in the front dash where the original radio had once been installed.

She burst out laughing when she saw the crocheted pink baby booties hanging from the rearview mirror. "You steal this from the senior center, or was it just abandoned, say in 1973?"

"Don't be fooled by what you see. This hunk of iron has plenty of modifications. Did half of 'em myself. And it's got run-flat tires. No spares needed for this little jewel."

"Little *jewel?* Are you sure you're not hallucinating from extreme fatigue?"

"Wait till she shows you what she's got." He had to struggle to open the passenger door and when he did, the metal squealed like an old iron gate. "A little lithium grease will take care of that," he mumbled.

As she got in, she was grateful to note that the bench seats were surprisingly comfortable, and the seat belts were in good shape. "Are you *sure* about this? Your truck seems to be running fine to me."

"That's not the problem. My pickup has been ID'd by whoever's after you. We're better off in a forgettable car—one without bullet holes."

"If that's the goal, then you've succeeded."

As he switched on the engine, her eyes widened. The deep-throated growl sounded more like a racing engine that the lawn mower putt-putt she'd expected to hear.

He glanced over and gave her a killer smile. "See? Trust me. A gentle touch and a little perseverance always works wonders."

His gaze slid down her slowly, leaving a trail of fire in its wake. Suppressing the delicious shiver that touched her spine, Dana took a deep breath and focused on the car. She was tired, that was all. Her brain was getting scrambled. "So where to now? Hopefully a place with a bed."

Seeing his slow grin, she nearly choked. "I meant a bed to sleep in. Alone. For hours."

As they reached the highway, the little sedan picked up speed quickly, giving them a remarkably smooth ride. For a long time neither of them spoke, each hiding behind the curtain of their own thoughts. He'd sensed that she carried a secret, but she also knew that he had his own as well. Those secrets were now creating a wall between them.

After a half hour, she glanced at him. "You never said where we're going, did you?"

"To a friend's place. No one will be able to find us there. It's just off the reservation."

She closed her eyes, intending just to rest, but in seconds she fell asleep.

SEEING HE HAD no cell phone service where they were, Ranger decided to stop and make a call on a public phone just outside a convenience store. As he glanced over at her, he realized that there was not much chance he'd wake Dana up when he got out of the car.

People reacted to stress differently. He was still amped up and angry that he'd been taken out when the kidnapping went down. He wouldn't have been able to sleep on a bet.

Ranger parked the car, then glanced over at Dana. She didn't even stir. Watching her as she slept, he felt a tug deep inside him, a gentling of sorts. He pushed the feeling back instantly. He couldn't afford the luxury of distractions now.

Moving as silently as the wind, he stepped out of the car, grateful that his door moved smoothly. Seconds later he heard his brother's voice on the phone.

"I need a sit rep," Hunter said, asking for a situation report. Ranger noted that his twin sounded tired, but alert.

Ranger updated him quickly. "Dana's holding something back. I suspect that she may have overheard what was forced out of our medicine man."

"If he'd thought that had happened, he would have sworn her to secrecy," Hunter said.

"Exactly. My guess is she's doing her best to honor that," Ranger replied.

"Is it possible she was involved in the kidnapping?"

"I can't be sure at this stage, but I doubt it," Ranger answered.

"Does she know about the Brotherhood of Warriors, or suspect you're one of us?" Hunter pressed.

"If she does, then she's pretty good at hiding it."

"We have to assume that the medicine man was tortured into giving them names. That means that some, or all of the brotherhood, may be in mortal danger. We've got to find out everything she knows about this. You've never failed to get whatever you want from a woman. What's so different about this one?"

"She's on a mission of sorts, and she appears to be very loyal. I'll stay on it and get back to you with anything I manage to learn."

After he hung up, Wind walked back to the car, gazing at the lights of the city to the east. The medicine man had known there was something special about Dana. He was sure now that was why *Hastiin Sani* had asked him for a ride from the school. He hadn't been above playing matchmaker.

Ranger's gaze drifted to the sleeping woman as he slipped back into the car. He'd never even been tempted to become a one-woman man, but Dana made him feel things he'd never felt before. He *wanted* to keep her safe, and not just because it had become part of his mission.

Dana stirred when he closed the door. "This car may look like a wreck, but these old bench-style seats are sure comfortable."

"You're just dead tired."

"I am, but I shouldn't have drifted off." She

looked around. "You stopped to make a call, huh? Cell phones are always iffy out here. Where are we going now?"

"To a house on Farmington's east side. But I want to make sure no one's tailing us, so we'll be taking the long way around on the back roads. Get more sleep if you can. We'll be there by first light."

Dana took a slow, deep breath. "I won't be able to go back to my job teaching on Monday unless all this is settled. Do you think it will be by then?" she added hopefully.

"Miracles happen, but the way things are going right now, I really doubt it."

"If they're after me because I can identify them, why don't we set them up using me as bait? They're sure to come for me and you guys can be ready and catch them. Then I'll be able to pass on the names and go on with my life."

"What names, and pass them off to whom?" he asked quickly.

Mentally thumping herself on the head, she came up with a quick answer. "I was talking about the names of students who won't be passing this semester. There are a lot of forms, calls and so on. Just teacher stuff." It was weak, but it was the best she could come up with quickly. She was too tired to even think straight anymore.

Frustration tore at him. He was almost certain

now that Dana had overheard at least some of the names of the Brotherhood of Warriors members. That was undoubtedly the information Trujillo had been after. But he couldn't be sure of anything except that Dana knew something, and he had to find out what it was.

"It's too early for a sting. The ones who come after you would only be the tip of the iceberg, hirelings like those we think are working for Trujillo."

"We need to take control of the situation, not just react. I've learned that in teaching. And don't think I'll stand passively by while you guys make all the decisions. It's not my nature to let others do my thinking for me."

Normally, ultimatums irritated the hell out of him, but he understood where she was coming from. As a kid, her life had been out of control. As an adult, Dana was determined to make sure that never happened again.

"We still have a lot of intelligence to gather before we can strike back," he said at last. Taking her hand, he held her gaze for a moment, then focused back on the road. "We're both having a problem trusting each other—except when it comes to mutual survival. You agree?"

She nodded.

"So let's simplify things. You know I can keep

us both alive. Will you trust my skills and decisions on security matters?"

She considered it, then nodded. "I will. And it's a good starting point toward building more trust."

"It's settled then."

They reached their destination just as the first rays of sunlight peered over the horizon. "We're here," he said. He hadn't looked over, and she'd yet to move a muscle, but somehow he'd known she was awake. There was a strange but powerful link between him and Dana.

The fifties-era residence was just outside the eastern city limits of Farmington, and there were no neighbors in the immediate vicinity. Fields, apple orchards and a fenced pasture with four horses butted up against a hillside of what seemed like a peaceful, ordinary ranch-style home.

Ranger retrieved the key from under a rock in a flower bed beside the porch, then unlocked the door for her.

As she stepped up to the threshold, Dana noted a tiny carving in the wood near one corner of the door frame. It looked like flames bounded by a circle. Before she could give it much thought, Ranger ushered her inside.

Chapter Seven

As they stepped into the comfortable-looking living room—with a contemporary brown leather sofa, matching love seat and recliner—the smell of fresh coffee greeted her.

"Coffee!" she said, ignoring the rest of the furnishings to focus on the sensory delight. Following her nose, Dana went directly to the kitchen and poured herself a cup from the large coffeemaker that had been left plugged in. Ranger put the car inside the garage, then came back into the kitchen to join her.

Several dishes were in the drain rack, dry, but the sink was still wet on the bottom. "Where are our hosts? They haven't been gone long, have they?"

"No, but they won't return till we leave. Safety precaution."

"You arranged for someone to give up their home so we could stay here tonight?"

"That's the way it works," he said, not elaborating.

She offered him some coffee, but he shook his head. "I'm going to try to catch a few hours of sleep."

"You're going to need more than that. You've been up all night."

"A few hours is all I need," he answered.

"Do you think anyone will mind if I take some food from the fridge?"

"No. We can take as much as we want," he said. Looking around, he spotted some fry bread in a plastic storage pouch on the counter beside a container of honey.

"Fry bread," she said, hungrily, following his gaze. "Care to share?"

He pushed the bag with the puffy, saucer-size pieces of golden skillet bread to the center of the table and placed the honey beside it. They each took a few pieces from the bag, then poured honey liberally over the tops.

"This tastes great," she said, licking the honey from her fingertips.

Hungry, they almost ate the entire contents of the bag.

"Now that my stomach's no longer empty, I'm going to take a shower," he said. "Then I'll catch some shut-eye."

"I like the way you set your priorities," she said, laughing.

He stood. "There's only one bedroom, so if we

stay the night, the bed is yours." He tilted her head up and brushed a crumb from her lip with his thumb. "But if we share the bed, I promise not to hog the covers," he added, his gaze holding hers.

The impact of that look melted her insides, but somehow she managed to find her voice. "No sharing. Behave."

"I behave very well in bed. I guarantee you'll wake up with a smile."

Her thoughts blurred and her skin flushed with an almost seductive warmth, but she managed to keep her voice steady. "You need that shower—a long, *cold* shower," she answered, her heart beating so fast she was close to having a heart attack.

He smiled, then walked away.

"Ranger?"

He glanced back at her. The look in his eyes was filled with just a touch of promise and sent a shiver racing through her. "I just wanted to ask you if I could use the phone…."

"Of course. Anything else? The shower here is large and modern. What are your feelings on water conservation?"

His gaze held a caress more intimate than should have been possible. For a brief eternity, Dana's brain stopped working.

He raised one eyebrow and smiled slowly.

"Don't think about it so much. Sometimes it's better to just follow your heart."

Suddenly aware she'd been holding her breath, she gasped, her face turning scarlet. "Go take your shower," she managed to say.

He came toward her, stripping off his shirt as he did. "But playing in the water can be *such* fun."

His bronzed, muscular shoulders and that beautiful strong chest were like a playground for consenting adults. Her fingers tingled as she fought the urge to touch him…to press herself against him.

Ranger held out his hand. "Come and play," he whispered.

The deep resonance of his voice traveled straight to her center. She wanted to…and it was crazy. She *never* acted on impulse. It just wasn't her. Yet, at that moment, following him made all the sense in the world to her.

She rose to her feet, then a loud explosion from somewhere down the highway rattled the windows. "What was that?" she asked, flinching.

He looked out the window, careful to avoid being seen from outside. "A backfire from a badly tuned car. Don't worry. I work around cars. I know the difference between that and a gunshot."

Breathing again, she averted her gaze. Ranger was too much of a temptation. It was like looking at hand-churned ice cream with whipped cream on top after a two-month diet. "Go take your shower. It's not too early to call my principal," she said, checking her watch. "I'll need to request an emergency leave of absence."

As he left the kitchen, Dana dropped back into her chair. She'd very nearly accepted his offer. What in the world had she been thinking? Well, maybe that was the problem. Around him, her brain cells automatically drowned in a sea of hormones.

After getting her leave of absence, Dana went out into the hall, stood there and listened. She could hear Ranger in the shower. Now was her chance. Finding a phone book, she searched for Daniel Runningbear, *Hastiin Dííl*'s legal, Anglo name. The directory included the Shiprock area, too, but she didn't find a listing. She had intended on calling the information operator next, but the water had stopped running in the shower.

She sat on the sofa, considering her next move, when something odd struck her. There was nothing personal in the rooms she'd seen. No photos were on the coffee table, bookshelves or the wall, and no letters or mail of any kind had been in the top cabinets or in the drawers she'd searched when she'd looked for the phone book. Although the place was meticulously clean and well cared for, it had all the warmth of a model home.

Curious now, she walked down the hall to

check out the rest of the house. The second bedroom had been turned into a study, judging from the desk and the extra bookshelves. Most of the volumes were nonfiction—southwest references covering everything from regional history to plant life. She turned on the small desk lamp and looked around carefully. Like the kitchen and living room, there was nothing in here that spoke of the house's owner. But she was getting distracted. Her top priority was finding something—anything—that might lead her to *Hastiin Dííl.*

She sat down at the desk and began to search through each drawer, but all she found were office supplies. Although she'd been careful to search in silence, when she looked up, she was startled to see Ranger standing by the door, watching her. He'd obviously just come from the shower, and was naked except for the towel wrapped low on his hips.

For a moment she couldn't speak. Her gaze drifted over him slowly and lingered over the gap that revealed everything from his left hip down.

He stepped over within arm's reach. "See something you like? Nothing to be scared of," he murmured, his eyes shadowed in the subdued light.

"I was just…" For some crazy reason she couldn't take her eyes off that gap in the towel.

"Yes, what *are* you doing?"

Her thinking became totally scrambled and she could have sworn she had a fever. "Hmm?"

"Tell me what you're looking for and maybe I can help," he said, his voice smooth and mellow. "You're all flushed. Something I can do?" he asked, stepping so close she could smell the fresh scent of the soap on his skin.

Her mouth fell slightly open as the towel parted a few more inches.

"You look like a woman who's ready to be kissed," he said, pulling her to her feet.

Before she could recover, his mouth was on hers. She'd expected fire and urgency, but his lips were gentle and coaxing, not at all demanding or aggressive. His tenderness melted her resistance.

Trembling in his arms, Dana gave him as much as he wanted to take. No one ever made her feel so wonderfully feminine. She ran her hand over his bare chest, loving the feel of him.

He nibbled her lips, tasting her, prolonging their pleasure. When she sighed, he traced her lips with the tip of his tongue, then deepened the kiss.

Need pounded through him. She was ripe for the taking. But he wanted more from her than mindless surrender. He wanted her to know what was happening between them, and choose him freely. Then he'd drive her wild and take everything she offered him. She'd remember what they'd shared then—remember *him*—for the rest of her days.

That thought stopped him cold. He'd never felt that way in his life. He'd had many women, and he'd enjoyed giving them pleasure and taking it, too. But this…it wasn't the same. His feelings for Dana…went deeper.

Ranger eased his hold and gazed down on her. "Woman, you're too tempting for your own good."

"So are you," she answered, reluctantly stepping out of his embrace.

He took a step back as well, and turned on the overhead room light. "What *were* you looking for in here?"

"Oh…just…." She scrambled for an answer. "I was searching for…paper…to write with, you know?"

"I'm aware of what paper's used for," he answered.

She saw the dangerous flicker in his eyes. He wasn't used to being lied to, and didn't like it one bit. She couldn't blame him. "A pad of paper, to be precise. I like to keep track of things."

"Used up all the pages in the notebook you have in your purse, huh? I think I saw a notepad on the shelf beneath the phone in the kitchen. Will that do?"

She nodded. She'd seen it, too, and one look into his coal-black eyes told her he knew it. "But that's there for a purpose. I didn't want to take something they were currently using."

"That's not a problem," he said with eyes that sliced through her.

As he walked out, she couldn't help but take one last look at him. No matter what he was wearing—or almost wearing—he was the stuff dreams were made of.

"There are some clothes in the bedroom closet— for men and women. Whatever's in there that fits you, you're welcome to take," he called out to her as he went back into the bedroom.

"Thanks, I'll go look once you're dressed," she said, opting for caution.

Her reaction to him made no sense at all. She'd met a lot of handsome, intelligent, eligible men over the years, but she'd never felt like this. Whenever Ranger was close her insides would hum with tension and her brain turned to instant mush. This just wasn't like her, and it had to stop.

Mentally using her best teacher's voice on herself, she went back into the kitchen and poured herself a cold drink. Dana walked back to the living room, forcing herself to relax, and her thoughts slowly cleared.

Just then he came out of the bedroom, shirtless. "I'm going to crash for a while. Make yourself at home, but stay away from the windows and don't step outside. If you hear anything unusual, come get me, though I'll probably hear it before you do. I'm a very light sleeper. And should the phone ring, let me get it. There's an extension in the bedroom."

"I'll keep watch," she said. "Rest easy."

Ranger went back into the bedroom and left the door open. While he rested she decided to turn on the small TV set in the living room, sound low, and catch the local morning news. There was coverage on the kidnapping and murder, but nothing new on the investigation.

After twenty minutes she tiptoed down the hall and looked in on Ranger. He was lying on top of the covers, wearing jeans only, and his deep, slow breaths indicated he was asleep.

Returning to the living room, she turned off the TV set and glanced around the room. There was something odd about this house. Maybe it was a safe house police agencies used to keep protected witnesses. It was possible, maybe even likely, that Ranger worked freelance for the tribe whenever they had someone who needed protection. That could have explained the carving on the door frame.

On top of some books stacked horizontally at the end of the bookcase, Dana spotted a laptop computer. Taking it from the shelf, she moved to the coffee table and sat cross-legged on the floor before it. It had a wireless Internet connection, so that meant that the router was somewhere in the house, though she hadn't seen one yet.

After turning off the speakers, Dana tried to get past the desktop display so she could access programs, but she kept getting a request for a password. She tried the obvious, starting with the word *password,* the name of the highway outside, the house number, Farmington and FPD, for Farmington Police Department. Nothing worked. The computer remained in the same opening screen. She continued, using terms such as protect and serve, witness, felony, police and police officer. Again nothing.

Dana sat back, rethinking her approach. She was missing something crucial. If this was intended for the use of whomever was scheduled to be at the house—in this case, Ranger Blueeyes—the password would be reset just for them. Her fingers flew over the keyboard as she typed in the name *Blueeyes.* After a short pause and a faint whirr from the hard drive, a new screen came up with the options to either log on to the Internet or search the files.

She decided to search the text and database files first. She soon discovered that the information seemed to focus on the Navajo tribe and was geared for use by a Navajo police officer.

Fortunately for her, she also wanted to know about Navajos—mostly one in particular, *Hastiin Dííl.*

There were reports on various issues the tribe was facing, but nothing that concerned or pertained to a *Hastiin Dííl*, or anyone named Daniel Runningbear.

Without another option, she decided to go on the Internet next. She could access more phone book listings from there. Using the phone itself would be too risky now. She logged on and, fortunately for her, the passwords for access had been stored in memory, so she didn't have to try to guess her way any further.

She started to type out *Hastiin Dííl*'s Anglo name, then stopped. This software usually stored a record of search words and sites visited, and she didn't remember how to disable or erase that information. Not wanting to leave a trail, she decided an indirect search was best.

Dana typed out the words *Navajo medicine men*. *Hastiin Sani* had been a medicine man, and men in his profession were highly regarded. It stood to reason that his successor in the Brotherhood of Warriors might be a medicine man, too. For all she knew, being a medicine man was one of the requirements for leadership.

Her search was slow and time-consuming, but she kept at it, intent on finding something that would lead her to *Hastiin Dííl*. She found a wealth of information about medicine men in general, but nothing specific. If there was a listing for medicine men anywhere, like physicians in the phone book, she couldn't find it.

Dana was about to give up when she found a link to an article about medicine hogans. She went to the site and read the piece, written by an anthropologist, who explained their different construction, like the fact that they were larger than other hogans and had no stovepipe in the center.

She also learned that medicine men usually frequented trading posts in traditionalist areas where their services were in high demand. These trading posts were also known to carry the materials the medicine men needed for the various kinds of Sings.

Unfortunately, this didn't get her any closer to *Hastiin Dííl,* though the site's map clearly delineated the more traditionalist sections of the rez. The problem was that the reservation itself was as large as several eastern states.

Dana sat back, lost in thought. She needed to nail down a smaller search grid. Assuming that the medicine man lived close to the Four Corners, maybe she could start by finding out more about the last Blessingway done in their area. If *Hastiin Dííl*'s name was mentioned, that might at least confirm that she was right in looking for a Singer.

Such events were often reported in the tribal newspaper. Dana was typing in the name of the newspaper when she heard footsteps down the hall and realized Ranger had woken up.

Moving with lightning speed, she shut down the computer and put it back where she'd found it. Then, spotting a book placed end out farther down on the bookshelf, she pulled it out and ran to the couch.

She was sitting back, pretending to be reading, when he sauntered in.

Chapter Eight

Ranger came in barefooted and bare-chested, wearing low-slung jeans. He looked completely relaxed and as drop-dead gorgeous as ever.

"You didn't sleep long," she said casually.

"I got nearly four hours," he said with a shrug. "That's all I need."

Dana looked at the clock in surprise. As it usually was whenever she was immersed in something, she'd lost all track of time.

"What you been up to?"

She shrugged. "I watched a little TV, then I decided to do a little light reading."

He picked up the book she held. "'Medicine Men, A Navajo Perspective.' That doesn't seem like light reading to me."

It took everything in her not to react. She'd only given the shelves a cursory look after seeing mostly a collection of popular fiction. Yet it was entirely possible that the information she'd tried so hard to find was sitting on her lap.

"I'm interested in all kinds of things," she replied, hoping it didn't sound as lame to him as it had to her.

He went to the laptop computer and, touching it, glanced back at her. "Still warm. This computer's encrypted. Did you try to get online?"

"Yeah, but the password got in the way."

He studied her expression for a moment, probably just to see if she squirmed, then picked up the laptop and carried it over to the coffee table. He sat down in nearly the same spot she'd chosen.

Ranger typed in a password and then another that took him to a screen she hadn't seen before. After two more passwords that appeared as asterisks on the screen, he reached a very official-looking government site. It was blue, with a gold emblem and shield in the center, and she thought it might have been the FBI's Web page. She moved closer to confirm, but he'd already reached yet another screen requesting a password.

"What are you doing?"

"Some creative information-gathering," he said.

"By hacking into...what, an FBI site?"

"I assume you referring to my status as a 'Full Blooded Indian,'" he answered. "Let's see what's new on the kidnapping suspects." He paused for a minute, reading what was on the screen, then continued. "The body they took from the cabin is still being processed at the Albuquerque OMI's office. They're checking dental records. Since the victim was wearing a Four Corners area high school ring, that should speed up the ID process."

Hearing several rapid beeping tones, he suddenly disconnected.

"What happened?" she asked.

"I had to log off. I got access through a site that spoofs my Internet address, but they have new software that can eventually backtrack to this location. If I'd stayed on, they would have had me."

"Looks like you've learned to cut some corners," she said. "So, assuming we aren't raided by the feds anytime soon, what's next on our schedule?"

"We lay low. The police advised me to keep you under wraps," he said.

She shook her head. "Bad idea. Growing up with my mom, I learned a lot about survival. The first rule is never wait around for others to do something on your behalf. That's a good way to become a victim."

Ranger gazed at her for a long time, then finally replied, "I understand what you're saying but, in this case, you *do* have someone working on your behalf. Going proactive now will only put you in the line of fire."

"I'm already there. I'm the only one who can

make a positive ID and the police still haven't arrested any of the kidnappers."

Ranger took a deep, slow breath. "Putting myself in Ignacio Trujillo's head, I've come up with an interesting theory. Want to hear it?" Seeing her nod, he continued. "Now that Ernesto's dead, Ignacio will want to take over his brother's business. But until he proves himself by avenging Ernesto, he won't be able to command any respect. He has to succeed or he's nowhere. This is more than a personal vendetta, so don't underestimate the threat he still poses to you."

"That only emphasizes the point I was trying to make. I'm in his sights no matter what I do. And after he gets the information he thinks I might have, I'll be of no further use to him."

"What kind of information would he be hoping to get from you?" he asked, pressing her. He was almost certain she'd heard *Hastiin Sani* give out names.

"By now he knows how close the medicine man and I were. So, for starters, I'm sure he'll want to know if he told me anything about the law enforcement officers who brought his brother down. He's hot on their trail."

"You don't have to worry about them. The officers who were involved in that operation have undoubtedly been informed of the danger," he answered.

"Maybe, but I remember reading that civilians

were part of that case, too. They were never identified by name, even by the police, but I understand
that they were responsible for supplying the
evidence used to get the arrests. We have no way
of warning them, and neither do the police if they
don't know their names. Something has to be
done—quickly. Those people are in danger."

Dana made her argument sound as logical as
possible. She had to find a way to get Ranger to
agree to let her out in public. That was the only way
she'd be able to find *Hastiin Dííl.*

He considered it for a long moment. "We'd have
better luck tackling that from a slightly different
angle. Maybe you can help me ID the people currently working for Trujillo. They'd be the ones he'd
call on to do his dirty work."

"The police wanted that from me, too, but I went
through several books of mug shots and they
weren't there."

"We could visit a few bars—the type of places
that attract people who need money and are willing
to do whatever's necessary to get it."

Ranger was playing things by ear. If he could get
Dana to trust him more, he'd have a better chance
of persuading her to stop holding out on him.

"Good plan. If we get lucky, we may even end
up running into one or two or his men," she said.

"Wait. Since some of them know what you look

like, we'll have to change our appearance. Or more to the point, you'll have to change *yours*. I was only seen from a distance, and didn't make the evening news—center stage—like you did," he said with a tight-lipped grin. "Go through the stuff in the bedroom closet. You'll find clothing, and wigs inside the boxes on the shelf. There's makeup, too, on the dresser. See what kind of a disguise you can put together."

"This place is looking more and more like an undercover officer's vacation home, or an actor's retreat," she said. When he didn't comment she added, "And what will you be doing?"

"I'm going to make a few phone calls and see if I can find out anything that might help us tonight."

As she went into the bedroom, her thoughts were racing. Ranger wasn't just some ex-military racing-team mechanic who moonlighted guarding witnesses for the police. With the knowledge and equipment he was using, it was beginning to look more and more like he was a plainclothes policeman…or maybe even a member of the Brotherhood of Warriors. The fact that he knew *Hastiin Sani* well enough to mourn over his death suggested a close association. But she needed facts, not guesses. His name hadn't been on the partial list she'd been shown.

It would have made matters easier if she could

have trusted Ranger and told him that what they had to do was find *Hastiin Díil*. But she'd promised *Hastiin Sani* not to divulge the information he'd given her to anyone except *Hastiin Díil*. And even if it hadn't meant breaking her promise, it would have still been risky telling Ranger anything. There was no way to predict his reaction once he learned that she was in possession of names no Anglo was supposed to have, especially because she'd never be able to prove how she got that information now that her friend was dead.

There were other reasons why that wouldn't work, too. She had a feeling he still wasn't totally convinced that she hadn't set up *Hastiin Sani*. He'd never take her to see *Hastiin Díil* under those circumstances. In fact, he might have taken steps to make sure she stayed as far away from *Hastiin Díil* as possible.

As those thoughts circled in her mind, she realized that there was also another serious problem with her trying to find the new Brotherhood of Warriors leader. She was currently Trujillo's target. If they were somehow followed, she'd be taking *Hastiin Sani*'s killers right to *Hastiin Díil*'s doorstep.

Of course she'd have a far better chance of going undetected if she traveled alone…but that wasn't going to happen, at least for now. The best she could hope for was that *Hastiin Dííl* had already gone into hiding and was well beyond everyone's reach.

When she'd given her word to pass the names on to *Hastiin Dííl,* she'd had no idea how complicated that would become. The names, for now, would have to remain locked away in her mind.

Dana opened the closet door, and saw the vast array of clothing inside. As Ranger had promised, there were plenty of styles to choose from, everything from formal evening wear to medical scrubs.

It took her forty-five minutes to complete a look that was totally unlike her own and still a good comfortable disguise. Wearing a short, dark-haired wig, a contrast to her shoulder-length copper-colored hair, black slacks and a hot pink long-sleeved T-shirt, she surveyed herself in the mirror. *She* didn't even recognize herself.

As Dana went back down the hall to show Ranger the results, she heard him on the kitchen phone. Judging from his end of the conversation, he was giving FBI Agent Harris an update.

Not wanting to interrupt him, she stayed well back. Standing to the side of the large bay window that faced the fenced backyard, she caught a glimpse of movement to her right. Suddenly a furry head with large ears poked out between the wooden slats of the fence. Then a small body followed, barely squeezing through. It was a domestic rabbit, probably the neighbor's pet. She smiled, thinking some child would soon come looking for the bunny.

Realizing in a heartbeat the danger of anything that might call attention to them—unfamiliar residents at the house—she stepped out into the yard through the side door.

It took only a few minutes to gather up the rabbit, which came right to her, and push it back through the space between the slats. She was down on her knees, having just placed a large rock in the gap so the rabbit couldn't get back through, when someone grabbed her arms firmly from behind.

She jerked her head back, hitting her attacker, and twisted away, rolling onto her back and kicking out. But her attacker was already too close. He evaded her legs and straddled her at the waist, pinning her arms down by her side.

She saw Ranger's face clearly and relaxed. But there was no immediate recognition on his face—just deadly intent. It was a side of him she'd never seen, and it was directed at her.

"It's me," Dana said quickly, forcing him to look past the heavy makeup and wig.

"Dana?" He stared, but didn't release her. "What were you doing out here?"

She could sense his anger and gave him a cold, level stare. "Isn't it obvious? I was trying to run away through a six-inch hole in the wooden fence. Now would you please get off me?" As she shifted her hips, she heard him bite back a groan.

"Why should I move? I like this position." He smiled slowly. It was one of those killer grins guaranteed to melt any normal female's heart.

"Because we're outside—in the open."

"Spoilsport," he said, then gave her a hand up. "Good disguise. But what were you doing out here crawling around on the grass?"

"I wasn't crawling around. I was returning the neighbor's bunny, who'd just sneaked through the fence. I didn't want anyone coming over who might start asking questions."

"So you were handling a security issue?" He grinned, and rubbed his chest where she'd whacked him with the back of her head.

"Yeah…that is, until I got assaulted." She could still feel the warm outline of his body against the cradle of her thighs. She sighed softly.

"Yeah, you do that to me, too."

"I have no idea what you're talking about. The grass was cold," she protested primly.

"Not anymore," he answered, hurrying back inside with her, then closing and locking the door.

Trying to focus her thoughts, Dana stared across the room at nothing in particular and forced her breathing to even out. His reaction to a perceived threat had been lightning fast and very effective. His training was obviously top-notch and the incident proved that she was in very good hands. And those hands...so rough, yet so incredibly gentle. She shivered.

"Stop fighting the attraction between us," he whispered in her ear. "Put yourself in my hands."

The temptation was overwhelming, but she stepped away from him. "Don't flatter yourself. I'm nowhere near that attracted to you. Now let me go fix this wig." She stormed down the hall, went directly to the bedroom and slammed the door shut.

Alone again, she plopped down on the edge of the bed and took a deep, steadying breath. She had no idea how to deal with her feelings for Ranger. She wasn't an innocent. Casual sex might have been an option if she hadn't been absolutely positive that there'd be nothing casual about it with Ranger. Her feelings, though undefined, were too strong, and went well beyond a physical attraction. Ranger simply wasn't the kind of man who brought out halfway emotions.

Finding grass stains on her wig and clothes, she opted for an entirely new disguise. Dana selected a long, blond-haired wig, jeans, and a light knit royal blue sweater. After adjusting her makeup to match her new look, she went back down the hallway.

When she drew close to the kitchen, she heard

Ranger speaking softly on the phone. The fact that he was deliberately keeping his voice down made her curious, and she stopped to listen.

"I'll find out what she's holding back and if she's really as innocent as she claims to be. But with Dana, if I rush it, I'll get nowhere. I need time to work."

Ranger's words squeezed the air out of her lungs. He hadn't been attracted to her at all. It had all been a game of manipulation—a way to soften her up and get her to lower her defenses. Seething, she walked back to the living room. But as her gaze fell on the laptop computer her anger gave way to logic…and a crushing sense of disappointment.

She couldn't really blame Ranger. Undercover cops worked to achieve a greater good and had to use whatever tools were at their disposal. Ranger was trying to find *Hastiin Sani*'s killers, and he'd known she was holding out on him. He'd simply done what he'd had to do.

As her anger faded, an unexpected sadness took its place, filling her, and draining her of all other emotions. Thinking that he really cared for her had given her comfort in a time of violence and fear. Now that comfort had been taken from her.

"There you are," Ranger said, coming out of the kitchen and giving her a once-over. "I think the dark-haired wig you had on before was a better disguise. You're going to attract attention no matter where you go because of your looks, but a light-haired wig in a community filled with mostly dark-haired women and men will make you stand out too much."

Earlier she might have thanked him for the compliment, but now she only saw it as insincere flattery. "I'll put the other one back on before we go to the bars tonight," she responded without expression.

"Good. For now, why don't you change into something loose and comfortable. Then I'll teach you some moves."

"Excuse me?" Her heart automatically started thumping overtime, but she forced herself to calm down. She couldn't allow him to play her like this.

"You need to know how to defend yourself in case someone comes after you and I'm not right there to help."

She'd already seen what the men after her were capable of doing. "I dislike violence, but that's a good idea."

"Just remember that this is about survival, not choice."

Dana nodded once, bracing herself. Like her mother before her, she'd learn to do whatever was necessary to keep going.

"There're some jogging pants and sweatshirts

in the chest of drawers in the bedroom. Pick a fit that'll give you maximum mobility and plan on a workout."

The promise of a workout with him teased her imagination but, with effort, she banished those feelings to a dark spot in her mind. Survival was all that mattered now.

By the time she joined him again, she'd already done some stretching exercises. It hadn't been to loosen her muscles, but more to focus her mind. Now, she finally felt ready.

"I've set things up for us in the garage," he said. "It's unheated and cold in there, but after a few minutes of heavy exercise, you won't notice it."

Dana followed him, her gaze straying across his shoulders and strong back. She'd seen how he'd made short work of those men who'd run them off the road. Ranger's body was well-toned and hard as steel. Suppressing a sigh, she trained her gaze on her shoes instead.

As they entered the two-car garage, she saw that he'd rolled out a large mat that covered half of the area not occupied by that deceptive-looking car. Ranger kicked off his shoes and she did the same.

"Okay, to the mat," he said.

They'd both stepped onto the soft surface when he suddenly took a step forward and swept her legs out from under her. She went down hard.

"Hey, I wasn't ready," she said, catching her breath. "That's your first lesson. *Never* lower your guard. Your enemy will always use it against you."

Chapter Nine

When Dana got back up, she kept her distance from him. "Bully. I won't repeat the mistake."

As he looked at her, he knew she'd be a quick study. Her eyes were focused now and she was watching him carefully. "Before we get to some of the basic moves, I have to teach you how to fall."

"I'll get my practice every time I hit the mat. Maybe you should teach me how to keep from falling."

Ranger didn't answer. In a dazzlingly fast move, he tried to sweep her legs out from under her again. This time, she jumped nimbly to one side.

"I told you, I don't repeat mistakes."

He gave her an approving nod. "That was *very* good. Now let me teach you a basic but effective defense move. Make your opponent *sing*."

He grabbed her from behind in a loose choke hold and pressed her against him. "*Sing*—first jam your elbow into your opponent's *solar* plexus," he instructed, bending her arm at the elbow and showing her how to aim. "The *i* is for *instep*. Stomp down hard on his foot with the heel of your shoe, then when he bends over, use your fist and slam it into the bridge of his *nose*. That's the *n*. The last part—and be careful now— is to take your fist and slam it hard into his *groin*. *Sing*. Get it?"

She nodded, then made a fist.

"Wait…let me see how you make a fist," he said.

She held it out. "A fist is a fist. So what?"

"Ever notice a boxing glove? There's a place for just your thumb. You only put your thumb on the inside of your fingers if you want to break it in a particularly painful way. Make a fist like this," he said, showing her how to place her thumb over her coiled fingers.

She imitated the position of his fingers, then went through the Sing exercise in slow motion.

"You need to practice this, because speed and surprise are your greatest allies," he said.

She loosened up, bending her neck to one side then the other. "Let's give it another try."

She went through the routine quickly, pulling her punches so she wouldn't connect and hurt him.

"The more speed you build up, the better off you'll be. Practice it in your head when you're not on the mat." He was pleased with how quickly she learned.

She was fast, but not so much as to make him suspect she might have been taught all that before.

He showed her a few other moves, then grew serious. "There are two kill moves I'd also like to teach you."

"Kill?" She shook her head. "No, I don't think I could kill anyone. Even under direct threat, I'd hesitate."

His admiration for her grew. She'd been brutally honest—with herself, and with him.

"You managed to fire that handgun yesterday in self-defense, didn't you? You'd be surprised what you're capable of when fear mixes in with the need to survive, or you're forced to protect an innocent."

Despite her protests, Ranger taught her how to deliver two fatal blows, one to the chest, and the other delivered to the nose. Although she learned both quickly, he could see she wanted to move on.

They spent the next two hours training in the garage. Though he'd thrown her to the mat several times, she always came back up ready to learn more. He had to hand it to her. Dana didn't give up, or hesitate to get right back into the fray.

"Okay, that's enough for now," he said at last. "Let's get something to eat. You might want to soak in the tub after lunch, too."

"I'm just catching on to some of this. Couldn't we train just a little longer?" she asked.

He shook his head. "You can't learn it all in one day, and tonight you'll have to be limber, not sore, in case something happens. I'll be within reach all night, but the bars I've got earmarked are rough places."

After eating a light lunch, Dana managed to talk him into giving her a few more lessons. This time, they mostly worked on techniques for breaking an opponent's hold.

Once he saw how tired she was, he moved away. "That's enough for today. You can think about what you've learned, and go over things in your head, but you need to rest."

"What are you going to do?"

"I have to access some Web sites and do more research," he answered. "After that, I may try to get a couple of hours sleep since I'm not sure when we'll get that chance again."

The day passed quickly. Around three, while he worked on the computer in the living room, she went into the bedroom and stretched out on the bed. Within minutes she was fast asleep.

When she awoke a few hours later, she found Ranger asleep on an easy chair he'd positioned between her and the door. Her first thought was that he'd been protecting her—putting himself between her and any potential intruder. But then another thought came to her. Maybe he'd just been making sure she didn't leave the house again without him knowing.

The thought annoyed her and she sat up. As she got off the bed, the mattress creaked slightly. Ranger's eyes suddenly popped open.

"I'm sorry. I didn't mean to wake you," Dana said.

"That's okay. I'm a just a light sleeper." He stood, then stretched.

By the time she'd found her shoes and slipped them on, Ranger had slid the chair back into place beside the wall and left the room.

"It's already eight. When do we leave?" she asked, going to join him in the living room.

"As soon as you get your disguise back on," he answered. He was gazing out the window toward the road. It was dark, but clear, and with the living room light still off he wasn't presenting a silhouette to anyone outside. "But there's a stop I want to make before we hit the bars. It may narrow our search. I'll tell you about it once we're on our way."

Dana freshened her makeup—she was wearing more than she ever would have outside a disguise—and picked out a short, jet-black wig she'd found in the back of the closet. When she looked in the mirror, she barely recognized herself.

They were in the car and on the highway ten minutes later, driving west toward the city. He looked over to appraise her, then back to the road. "You look sexy," he said with a quirky half smile.

Her heart did a little dance, but she quickly checked herself. She knew it was all an act. "It must be the new wig. It's completely black, no lighter highlights anywhere. It changes my whole look."

"No, it's the way you fill out those tops…and the jeans, too."

"The same can be said about you," she answered.

He burst out laughing. "Thanks, darling. It's good to know I'm appreciated. Now if you'd let me show you my appreciation in a more…tangible way."

"Shouldn't we be concentrating on what we have to do next?" she chided in her best teacher's voice.

"You're too wound up," he said quietly. "Try to relax," he said, glancing at her lap.

That's when she suddenly realized that she'd bunched up the bottom hem of her sweater into her fists. "Oops. Stage fright, I guess."

"Stop worrying. I've got your back," he said, his voice soft as a summer breeze.

As their gazes met, she felt herself drowning in those dark eyes that promised far more than she could accept. "Neither one of us has put all our cards on the table, Ranger. You don't trust me, and I can't say I trust you, either. We can't go beyond that."

He looked back at the highway, where traffic was starting to pick up as they got closer to Farmington. "You can trust one thing. I won't let anything happen to you," he answered.

"That's because you need me to ID the medicine man's killers," she said, determined not to let him see how much that admission hurt.

"That's one reason. But there are others." When they stopped at a traffic light, he cupped her chin and made her look at him. "Your own instincts tell you that there's more between us. Trust *yourself.*"

She tore her gaze away. Her instincts... They told her that she wanted him and he wanted her, that there was more than just a physical attraction between them. But she'd heard how he was manipulating her to get information.

"We're about to stick our necks way out tonight. I've got to know that I can trust you and you've got to believe I've got your back. If we aren't in complete agreement on that much, our chances of success are slim."

"No problems there," she said. "Now tell me where we're going first."

"About a year ago we hired a guy at Birdsong Enterprises who turned out to be a thief. He was caught stealing tools from the shop. But he and I got along, and though I had to fire him, there were no grudges. I learned later that the guy's got a bit of a gambling problem and is always looking for a way to make a few quick bucks. If I approach him just right, he may give us a few leads."

"So we're going to his home?"

"No. There's a tough-man competition, in this case an illegal cage fight, that he attends regularly. I'm guessing we'll find him there. But brace yourself. It's brutal, with few rules, all for a cash prize."

Out of all the recreational sports she'd hoped never to see, this one topped the list. "Okay," she said, managing to keep her voice steady. "Just don't be surprised if I throw up on somebody."

"You don't have to watch. Just stick close to me—no matter what. Got that?"

"Not a problem." Dana tried to prepare herself. She even hated school fights, pulling boys with bloody noses off each other. But she'd do what had to be done. Somehow, she hoped.

They arrived less than twenty minutes later. The fight was being held in a large metal warehouse located in an industrial section just southeast of downtown. Vehicles lined the curbs on both sides of the street, and Dana could see mostly young men, some with beer bottles in hand, walking toward the structure.

"It's packed," she said. "I never thought so many people would be interested."

"Yeah, it's popular, and most who come bet heavily on their favorite fighters. The promoters switch locations all the time to avoid getting raided, and there are rumors that officers are being paid to look the other way. I got tonight's location earlier from a source at my workplace."

Three big goons with handheld radios stood beside the only entrance, a double door at the side of the structure above a small loading dock. After handing over a forty-dollar admittance fee for the two of them, they walked into the two-story structure. Judging from the signs outside, it had been a former maintenance garage for oil service company vehicles. But whatever oil smell might have lingered was overwhelmed by the odor of dust, beer, stale tobacco and sweat.

Hundreds of people were crowded around a hexagonal, wire-covered framework atop a makeshift stage in the center of the big room. Two slightly overweight men were swinging wildly at each other with bare fists. Between the grunts from the center of the ring, and the ebb and flow of voices from the crowd, the place literally vibrated with the rawness of underground life.

Ranger held her hand tightly, and when he glanced over at her, she was looking down at her feet. He was certain she'd never seen anything even remotely like this.

Dana didn't say a word, though she would have had to shout to be heard, and he couldn't think of anything to say that would help her now. Finally she looked up, holding her head high at last, and gave him a stiff-lipped smile.

Ranger switched his gaze to the people around and ahead of them, ignoring the shouts, raised beer bottles and the money being waved around. He was searching for Jimmy Brownhat.

The people were crowded elbow to elbow around the cage. Ranger surveyed the faces slowly and methodically. Then, at long last, he spotted Jimmy across the room, standing on a pallet against a wall, high enough for an unobstructed view. He was shouting encouragement to one of the fighters.

As the crowd roared almost in unison, Jimmy looked away, shaking his head. Judging from the groans among the cheers, one of the fighters had either just delivered a knockout punch, or his opponent had thrown in the towel. Jimmy jumped off the pallet, and started walking in the direction of the entrance.

"He's leaving. We need to catch up to him before he disappears," Ranger said, elbowing his way through the mass of people.

The press of the crowd forced Ranger to switch directions quickly, but as they went through a maze of angry losers, he felt Dana's hand slip away from his. Ranger turned around, but before he'd even taken a step, three people pushed in between them.

Looking around, Dana waved him on. "Go! I'll catch up."

Dana changed directions, heading for the closest open area. Just as the mass of people around her began to thin, someone grabbed her arm.

"Hey!" she yelled, turning around. A tall, dark-haired man with a tattoo on his arm held her in a painful, viselike grip.

"Come on, baby," the man said, yanking her so close she could smell the beer and tobacco on his breath. "If you're looking for company, you're in luck. Let's meet my brother over by the door, then take a walk to my van. The three of us can rock the night away."

Terror gripped her. *Hastiin Sani* had died trying to keep the others from hurting her. Now Ranger would be forced to take on two drunks. She was certain it would happen once he spotted her being strong-armed outside. Anger swelled inside her. No one she cared about would ever again be harmed because of her.

She looked up into the man's eyes and smiled. "Sounds like fun!"

He eased up on his grip, and she kicked him hard in the knee. He howled in pain, and as he bent over, she chopped down on the side of his neck with the heel of her right hand. Her aim was off and she mostly struck him on the back, but the force of the blow sent him down to one knee—the injured one.

With a scream of pure rage, the man hurled himself at her. She sidestepped the tackle and stuck out her foot, tripping him. His momentum dropped him facedown on the floor.

"Look, I don't want any trouble," she said, backing away. But it was too late. Without a fight in the center ring, everyone's attention had suddenly shifted to the rear of the room—to her and the man she'd just knocked down.

"Fight, fight, fight," the chant started up, like kids in the schoolyard during recess.

"Twenty dollars on the babe," someone yelled from behind her, followed by a chorus of laughter.

The drunken, wannabe rapist outweighed her by at least one hundred pounds. He wasn't going to back away, not with all eyes on them. She looked around for Ranger, but three men were struggling to hold him back. He'd get away eventually, but for the next minute or two she was on her own.

The man howled with rage and charged at her like a bull. She tried to step aside at the last minute and trip him again, but this time he was ready. He grabbed her arm as he went by, spinning her around. They nearly fell together, but somehow he kept them on their feet, yanking her back against him by the hair.

Pinned to a man with biceps the size of a side of beef, she panicked. She struggled wildly to break free, scratching him on the face but that only made him angrier.

"Got you now, witch!"

Then she remembered her lessons with Ranger. His arm had been in the same place. Dana sagged as if giving up. Then, as his hold eased somewhat, she rammed her elbow right into the man's midsection as hard as she could and stomped on his instep with the heel of her boot, putting everything she had into it. The man yelped in pain, letting go as he stumbled back.

"I'm not done yet," she yelled, arms up in a defensive stance. The drunk staggered away, then disappeared into the crowd.

"Hey!" Someone behind her called out.

Remembering that her opponent had a brother, she spun to face the new threat. That's when she saw that Ranger had managed to break free.

"Give it up for the lady," a tall, thin man shouted from the edge of the crowd.

As the people laughed and cheered, Ranger scooped her up, threw her over his shoulder and hurried out the side door. The novelty over, the crowd's attention quickly shifted to the next two combatants climbing into the elevated cage.

Once they were outside in the parking lot,

Ranger quickly did as she asked by setting her back down, and they hurried back to the car.

Ranger finally spoke as they were racing down the street in the Ringer. "So much for staying low-key."

"Hey, at least my wig stayed on. Good thing I pinned it in place."

He stared at her. "That's *all* you have to say?"

Dana opened and closed her fist. It hurt like crazy, but she was pretty sure she hadn't broken anything. "What else could I do with my body-guard AWOL? And, just for the record, I didn't appreciate that caveman routine when we left. It's not a comfortable method of travel."

"But effective. Nobody wanted to have 'the babe' thrown at them. We got a wide berth." He looked at her, and then burst out laughing.

She glared at him for a moment, then finally started laughing, too.

"I can't believe I lived through that," she said at last, tears of laughter running down her face.

"Crazy Louie's one mean drunk. But you ate him alive," he said, admiration in his gaze. "But why didn't you just pretend to go with him? I'd have seen what was going on before you ever reached the door. Didn't you think I could handle him?"

"It wasn't that, or even that he'd said his brother was going to join him and you would have been outnumbered. I made up my mind right then that no one else would ever be hurt on my account," she said, then added, "even if my hand is black and blue in the morning."

Chapter Ten

Once they were a safe distance away, he pulled to the side of the road. "Let me take a look at your hand," Ranger said.

She flinched when he touched her fingers. "It hurts. Go easy. It was like hitting a brick wall when I got his backbone instead of his neck."

"Nothing's broken," he said after a moment. "At least you remembered how to make a fist."

"I remembered everything you taught me, but he ran before I could get to the *N* and *G* of that Sing move. Too bad. The guy could have used a good kick in the *G*."

"You're one helluva woman, Dana." Before she could even think, he pulled her into his arms and kissed her. Feeling her melt against him, he pressured her lips to part, then tasted her slowly, deliberately, changing the angle of the kiss only to deepen it.

His fingers skimmed the column of her throat. Her pulse was beating wildly, and her soft sighs drove him crazy. With a groan, he let her go. He'd take her right there and then if he didn't cool off. Whatever crazy feelings drew him to Dana were real and more powerful than he'd ever dreamed.

"Why…" she whispered breathlessly, running the tip of her tongue over her lips. She could still taste him.

Ranger settled into the driver's seat, keeping his distance. "Wanting you is making me a little crazy," he warned, an edge in his voice.

The expression of disappointment on her face was almost his undoing and he had to look away. "Let's go to the house. You need to change clothes. Then we'll set out again."

SHE SHOWERED QUICKLY and changed clothes. The sweater had been smeared with Crazy Louie's blood and was torn in places. She tossed it into the trash. She'd buy its owner another as soon as her life got back to normal.

Normal…would she ever have a normal life again? Her feelings for Ranger changed everything. Thoughts of him simmered in her mind, mingling with hopes and dreams. They persisted, even though she knew that giving in to those emotions would only distract and endanger both of them.

Dana joined him in the living room minutes later. As she saw his gaze traveling slowly down her frame, she had to work hard to squelch the flutter in her stomach.

"That brown, long-haired wig changes your looks completely. It's perfect. Even if we run into someone who was at the fight, chances are you won't be recognized."

She held out her swollen hand. "This'll give me away. It's already starting to turn blue—even though I put makeup on it."

He started to take her hand, then abruptly changed his mind and turned away, but not before Dana saw the flash of fire in his eyes. There'd been a burning there, a hunger her soul recognized.

As they walked out to the car, Dana remained a discreet distance away from him. He was still too much of a temptation. "Where to next?"

"The Back Alley. It's a bar on the other side of town."

She cringed. "More fights…."

"No, not at this place. The bouncers keep everyone under tight control. At the Back Alley the police are the enemy—and everyone has cop radar."

"So what's the plan once we're inside?" she said, getting the idea fast.

"You're my old lady, and I'm muscle who'll do anything for money. With luck, we'll run into whoever hires for Trujillo. Then we can check for known associates and that might give us a lead to the kidnappers. The tribal police believe the kidnappers were local talent and I happen to agree."

"Okay, I'm ready," she said.

He gave her the once-over again. "Let me do the talking. There's something about you...a gentleness, a softness... It makes you stand out."

She gave him a long look. "How many butts do I have to kick before you'll give me some credit, huh?"

He laughed. "Play the cards you've got. Stick with the naive look. They'll underestimate you."

"Did you...at the beginning?"

"I wasn't sure what was on the inside, but I liked the packaging. Still do," he added in a rich baritone voice.

His words had felt like an intimate caress. "And do you know what to make of me now?" she asked in a whisper-soft tone.

He said nothing for several long moments. "You're getting under my skin, schoolteacher," he said at last. "I'm not sure if that's a good thing or bad, but it's a fact."

It was more John Wayne than John Keats, but his words gave her a powerful rush. Yearning...she understood that emotion better now than she ever had before.

They approached the bar, which was located on a narrow side street in east Farmington a short time later. Ranger took a parking spot close to the door as another car was leaving. "Take a good, hard look at the people inside. If you see anyone we might be interested in, let me know."

Once inside, Ranger chose a table that allowed them to keep their backs to the wall and still get a good look into the room.

"I recognize the bartender, and he knows I'm not law enforcement. For a Jackson, he'll answer a quick question or two.

"Order whatever's on tap for me, and something for yourself, while I go over to talk to him." His eyebrows rose as he added, "Think you can stay out of trouble?"

"If you can, I can. Just don't make me have to come over and save your behind," she added.

He laughed. "Okay, sweetheart. You've got yourself a deal."

Dana watched as he joined the bartender, then struck up a conversation. Though deep in discussion, Ranger would glance back at her often, making sure she was okay, and the gesture—and its intent—made her feel good.

A waitress in tight jeans and western-style shirt came over to take her drink order.

"Dana, I thought that was you! I *love* your wig," she said.

Dana shifted her gaze and recognized the pretty

young woman instantly. Jenny Miller worked as a teaching assistant at the school.

"Shhh," Dana warned. "Nobody's supposed to recognize me."

"Keeping a low profile after being kidnapped? I don't blame you," she whispered, sitting down on the chair beside her. "We were all told you'd had to take a leave of absence for your own protection. But if you don't want to be recognized, I better give you a heads-up. Coach Martin is here hoping to hook up tonight. He's always had a thing for you, and that wig might just turn him on."

Dana groaned. "Just what I need." Looking in the direction Jenny pointed, Dana saw Martin flirting with a busty blond waitress. "Oh, good! I think he's already making his move."

"That's probably just the first girl of the evening for him. Stay in the shadows. I'm engaged now, so hopefully he won't try to hit on me, but Martin seems to like going from one woman to the next... kinda like the guy you came with."

"You know Ranger?" Dana asked.

She nodded. "Sure. Heck, half the women around here have made a move on him. He's a lot of fun, and a good guy, but he's definitely not relationship material. I dated him for a while two years ago, but it didn't work out. Same old story. I was getting serious—he wasn't," she said with a sigh.

Dana hadn't been prepared for the news, though all things considered, she should have expected something like this. Ranger was smooth and that usually came from experience. A man with his looks and confidence was bound to have more than his share of opportunities.

"But don't worry," Jen continued. "Even when he stops calling or coming around, he'll let you down easy. Ranger's decent about the whole thing. Once he knew I was starting to get serious, he ended it."

"Who's he dating these days?" she asked, unable to resist.

"Last I heard, he was seeing three or four women. One of them is Linda McFadden, the anchor for channel eight news."

The local cable news celebrity, besides having a degree in journalism, had curves in all the right places. Her early claim to fame had been as New Mexico's selection for a national beauty contest. "If he's interested in her…"

"You think he won't take more than a passing look at you?" Jenny said, finishing Dana's thought. She shook her head. "First, you're as pretty as Linda, and a heck of a lot smarter. But Ranger isn't attracted just by looks. He met Linda while dating Chloe Vargas, the weather girl."

Chloe was Linda's polar opposite, and went counter to the old stereotype of the "all looks and no brains" weather girl often seen on major news outlets. Chloe was plain-looking and her only noticeable curves were around her bottom. Yet her intelligence and humor gave her an on-air sparkle that was responsible for her having landed the job.

"As I said, Ranger likes women," Jen said in response to Dana's surprised look. "No, let me amend that. Ranger *loves* women. All sizes and shapes," she said. Lowering her voice to a conspiratorial whisper, she added, "He and I never made love, but I've heard from a woman who shall remain nameless that once you've been with him, no one else quite measures up."

That was possibly the last thing Dana needed to know. Her imagination had been working overtime. Now it was on hyperdrive.

"My source says that Ranger definitely knows how to use what nature gave him…and then some."

Dana sighed openly. Despite all the reasons against it, he'd always been a temptation. Now it would be worse. But she *had* to stay focused.

Jenny turned, hearing her name being called, and saw the bartender motion to her with a toss of his head. "I better get back to work," she said, taking Dana's drink order.

As Jenny hurried away, Dana spotted Martin across the room, deep in conversation with a stunning black woman who'd just taken a seat by the bar. When he looked up, Dana ducked quickly, pretending to be looking in her purse. When she surfaced again, she saw that he'd moved with his new friend to an area where the patrons were playing darts.

Dana smiled with relief, but a man seated by himself two tables down smiled back, thinking her gesture had been directed at him.

The man, with wavy black hair and a big gold chain clearly visible in the spot where he'd left two buttons of his shirt undone, grabbed his drink and sauntered over. "Why in the world would any man leave a pretty lady like you all alone?"

She glanced at Ranger, but he was still talking to the bartender. When she turned back, "Wavy Hair's" hand was on the table, still holding his drink. She could see a pale stripe around the left ring finger of the wannabe Romeo.

Thinking fast, Dana reached into her purse and brought out her small notebook and pen, then looked him squarely in the eye. "I'm a reporter for the *Farmington Journal*. I'm doing a piece for our lifestyles section on pickup lines men use when stepping out on their wives."

"Oh…well, I'm not married so I can't help you. Good luck with the story," he said, picking up his drink and moving away quickly.

She was still chuckling, sipping the rum and cola

Jenny had delivered, when Ranger finally joined her. "What was that all about," he said, picking up his glass and taking a deep swallow of beer.

"I'll tell you later. What did you get?"

"Not much, except that Trujillo himself has been here several times in the past few weeks, which was a surprise to me. Apparently, he started from scratch when he put his team together. But word's out now, and those looking for work go straight to him. Have you seen any faces you recognized?"

"None of the men I've seen tonight were involved in the kidnapping."

After they each took another swallow from their drinks, they decided to leave. They were halfway to the door when Jenny came rushing up.

"Hey, Ranger," she said, beaming him a smile. "Barry said you're looking for men Trujillo might have hired?" Seeing Ranger nod, she continued, her voice much lower now. "He's got at least one guy on the payroll these days helping him screen out potential employees. The guy was in just last week. He wears some kind of uniform."

"Military?"

"No," she answered. "Works for the city, like in a shop. I recognized the city patch on his sleeve, but I was at the wrong angle to see the details."

"Think hard, Jennifer," Ranger said. "Can you give us anything more?"

She blew out a breath. "Just that the uniform was brown, like UPS, only a shade or two lighter. He was wearing a matching cap, too."

"He could be in any of their shops, a utilities inspector, or even drive a disposal rig. Was he short or tall, fat or skinny?" Ranger pressed.

"He was sitting down. All I can tell you for sure is that he looked fit."

"Like a weight lifter?" Ranger asked.

"No, more like a runner. He had a nice smile, too."

Dana didn't have to look at Ranger to feel his exasperation. "What made you notice him?" Dana asked, playing a hunch.

"That's easy. Although he was dressed like a working man—no tie or white collar—he had expensive tastes. You know how I collect old-style money clips cause they remind me of my dad?"

Dana nodded.

"His looked like a real antique. It must have cost him a fortune. I was pea-green with envy when he peeled off a twenty for his tab."

"A money clip?" Ranger repeated.

"Yeah, really beautiful. He held it out for me to take a closer look when he saw I was interested. It was gold and engraved with an intricate design, maybe an initial. And he had a gold watch that must have set him back five hundred bucks."

After getting a quick description of the guy—unfortunately Jenny had spent her time looking at the money clip and watch, and couldn't even remember the color of the man's eyes—they left the bar.

A few minutes later they were underway. "As far as leads go, that's a strange one, but I think I know how to follow it up," Ranger said, turning toward a residential area. "We need to see a friend of mine who works for the city." He picked up the cell phone. "Let's just hope she's home. If I remember correctly, Saturday's her favorite night out."

"A former girlfriend, and you still feel free to call and ask to drop by at this hour?" she asked, surprised. The fact that he'd remained friends with more than one woman from his past spoke well for Ranger.

"Do I detect a trace of jealousy in your voice?" he teased.

"In your dreams, guy."

His grin widened. "Be careful what you wish for. My dreams are all X-rated."

Her flesh prickled as her imagination fueled her already awakened desire. "Focus on business," she said for her own benefit as well as his.

"You *are* my business."

"The day I'm not, then we'll talk more about our dreams," she said softly.

"Count on it," he answered with a nod. "And Dana?" She looked back at him. "I always keep my word."

Chapter Eleven

The ranch-style home, complete with stables and a riding area, was on a multiacre lot on the northwest outskirts of Farmington. Tall bluffs lined each side of a narrow valley that led north toward the foothills of the San Juan Mountains.

Maria Charley was a slender, beautiful Navajo woman in her early forties with petite, oriental features. She placed a platter of fresh fruit in front of them, then sat in a chair across from the leather western-style couch.

"It's good to see you," Maria said, looking at Ranger. "I hope he's treating you well," she added, looking at Dana. There was no animosity in her tone or her expression.

"We're just getting to know each other," Dana answered cautiously.

Maria gave her a puzzled look, making Dana suspect she wasn't used to getting lukewarm responses from Ranger's girlfriends.

Dana was tempted to explain that they were simply business partners, but then changed her mind. Ranger was here to get information, not give it out.

"I gather this isn't a social visit," Maria said, giving Ranger a curious look. "You sounded… tense on the phone."

"I'd almost forgotten how observant you are," he said.

"It helps when you're an accountant. So tell me what brings you here," Maria answered with a tiny smile.

"I need your help," he said directly.

"No problem. What do you need?"

Her response surprised Dana. Maria hadn't even hesitated. Jenny had told her that Ranger had a way with women. Maybe the memories he created were worth the price of heartbreak.

Dana found the thought intriguing…and disconcerting. It was a little scary to feel herself so drawn to a man who should have come with a warning label—or maybe a disclaimer.

"You've worked for the city for years now. What department wears brown uniforms?" Ranger asked.

Maria thought about it, then shook her head. "The only departments I can recall off the top of my head are sanitation and maintenance, but I'm sure there are others, too," she said, then added, "Come to think of it, animal control officers wear that color. One of their people came by last week and captured a stray dog that had been getting too close to my neighbor's miniature horses."

"Roughly, how many people total are we talking about in that color uniform?" Ranger asked.

"Fifty, more or less," she said after a pause. "But I won't be able to give you anything more concrete until Monday."

"We're looking for a guy who wears a brown city uniform, moonlights and isn't too picky about the jobs he takes on," he added, then gave her a description of the man Jennifer had seen.

"That physical information will rule out the women and a good number of the men. I'll see what I can find out."

"Before Monday?" Ranger pressed.

"Okay," she said with a sigh. "Before Monday, if I can, but I'm not promising anything."

After accepting something to drink and enjoying some small talk, Ranger and Dana left.

"You're very quiet all of a sudden," Ranger remarked as they headed back west toward the reservation.

"You and Maria get along great. I'm surprised you're not still dating."

"We're friends. That's all we ever were."

"Has there ever been anyone really special in your life?"

He paused thoughtfully, then finally nodded. "A few times," he said, then correcting himself added, "Twice."

"What happened?"

"My first love jilted me," he said somberly.

Surprised, she turned to look at him.

"Her parents gave her a horse for her twelfth birthday—and after that, she never had time for me."

She scowled at him. "I was being serious!"

"Me, too," he teased.

"Okay, what about your second love?"

He smiled slowly at her. "That's still a work in progress."

Her heart did a quiet somersault and there was a little hitch in her breath. Realizing from his expression that he was only too aware of his effect on her, she glanced away.

"Where to now?" Dana asked at last.

"We've stirred up enough trouble tonight. I think it's time to pack it in."

"So we're going back to the safe house?" she asked.

He shook his head. "Our best chance is to stay on the move. I have another place in mind. But I need to make a call first and my cell's not getting a signal here," he said, placing the phone back down on the seat.

Stopping at a gas station, he walked to the pay

phone outside and dialed. She strained to hear, but she couldn't make out much.

Seeing him keeping his back to her, and his voice lower than normal, forced her to face a difficult fact. He still didn't trust her, but in all fairness she couldn't blame him. Ranger's priority was to find *Hastiin Sani*'s killers, and he mistakenly believed she was withholding information that could help him do that.

They would never really be able to work together. That much was clear. It was time for a drastic change of plans. There was only one way for her to keep her promise to *Hastiin Sani* and not endanger *Hastiin Dííl*. The first chance she got, she'd have to get away from Ranger. Trujillo and the others wouldn't be on the lookout for a woman traveling alone, not now. She'd change her appearance and complete the task on her own.

He joined her a moment later and they drove west through Shiprock and then headed on toward the Arizona border. They turned south again a short time later and drove down a narrow highway, then onto a graveled road that went past a trading post she didn't recognize.

Dana concentrated, trying to get her bearings. All around them were piñon- and juniper-covered hills, and with only the moon to light her surroundings, she was having very little luck.

"Where are we? I know we were heading toward Beclabito for a while, but then we went south again, right?"

"We're close to the Arizona state line, in a mostly traditionalist area. There are very few modern amenities out here, and that keeps away those who require air-conditioning and telephones. I've always loved this part of the rez myself. Open country is part of every Navajo…though some forget."

"It's beautiful, but life out here would be hard," she said softly, seeing a stunted piñon tree growing precariously on the side of a cliff.

"It can be. Mother Earth nourishes The People but also tests us constantly. It's our beliefs that keep us strong. In the *Diné Bekayah*, Navajoland, the mountains have names and they watch over the *Diné*. The Holy People are with us as Wind, Lightning, Thunder, Sky and Rain. We know which offerings will appease them and how to call down their blessings. Living in balance and harmony, honoring that all things are connected, we walk in beauty."

His voice resonated with a deep love for his tribe and this sometimes inhospitable land. Ranger was a man with loyalties that went deeper than the eye could see. "Your heart is here. I wish I had that sense of home. I envy you that."

"I'll share mine with you," he said and covered her hand with his.

Despite all the barriers she'd put in the way to protect her heart, his words and the gesture touched her. Then, slowly, rationality returned. Ranger was a man on a mission.

She pulled her hand away and shifted in her seat. "Where *are* we going?"

"I'm taking you to my family home. My parents are both gone and the house stands empty, but my brother and I have maintained it. We use it from time to time to go hunting and fishing, or just to get away."

She wondered how many other women he'd taken up here as well.

As if reading her mind, he added, "I've never taken anyone up there," he said. "I've known many women," he added slowly. "That's hardly a secret. But this place says too much about who we were as a family. It's a simple place that means a lot to me and I didn't want anyone passing judgment on it. But from what I know about you, I think you'll be able to see with more than just your eyes."

He sounded sincere, but she knew that his goal was to gain her trust, and find out everything she knew. Opening up to her, revealing personal matters, could have been part of his strategy.

"You grew up with traditionalists?" she asked.

He nodded. "It wasn't an easy life, but we worked together. Our family was very close. Everything about our old home reminds me of who I was once. Memories are everywhere."

"But you're taking me…out of necessity, or choice?"

"A little of both," he answered after a brief pause. "But I could have chosen other places. I…wanted you to see it." He gave her a quirky half smile. "An act of faith, if you will."

"In me, or in our journey to find justice for a mutual friend?" she asked, then regretted it instantly.

"If you have to ask, then you won't believe my answer."

"I'm sorry. I didn't mean to sound so hard and analytical. Speaking about the past always makes me uncomfortable. For the most part, my own memories are something I'm saddled with, not ones I cherish. The only thing I learned back then is that I can survive almost anything." Including the loss of…possibilities, she added to herself, still looking at him.

It was two in the morning by the time they arrived. The small log cabin lay within a clearing surrounded by tall pine trees, and mostly hidden from view.

"Is someone here?" she asked quickly, seeing the back end of a vehicle parked by the side.

"No. My brother and I keep that truck here for the times when the rain or snow takes out the roads. That old Chevy has a low gear we call Granny, and it never gets stuck in the mud. The more modern trucks and cars can have some real problems out here when it rains."

The cabin didn't look nearly large enough to fit four people, but even from outside, it gave off a welcoming feel, and she said so.

"My dad, my brother, and I built this place practically from scratch using the trees we had to clear away to protect us from forest fires. There was just enough space for all of us. With only a few rooms, it was a lot easier to heat in winter, and much more airtight than a traditional hogan. My mother grew vegetables in the back and canned as much as she could, and our water came from a spring up against the hillside. There's a small lake just a mile from here, so we had fish when we needed them. There was always food on our table."

Reading her expression, he added, "We never thought of ourselves as poor. In all the years we lived here, we never lacked anything important."

"What happened to your parents?"

Ranger's voice grew hard. "My father…worked for the tribe. He was killed on the job."

She wondered if his father might have been in the Brotherhood of Warriors, but for obvious reasons, it wasn't something she could bring up. Before she could ask anything more, Ranger continued.

"My mother passed away six months later. She

drove away one day, left the car parked on the side of the road and walked off into the desert, like our traditionalists often do."

She stared at him, stunned, trying to understand what he'd just said. "She...*walked* off?"

He nodded. "She'd been diagnosed with an advanced form of cancer. Traditionalists don't want to die at home. That would taint the house for the family. They go off someplace by themselves where their *chindi* can't harm anyone. It's our way, and Mom was ready. She wanted to be with my father."

Dana tried to understand the mind-set of someone choosing to die alone out in the middle of nowhere. No matter how hard she tried, she couldn't quite wrap her head around the concept.

"It's a final act of love...and sacrifice," he added, as if guessing her thoughts.

She suddenly understood. His mother's last act had been one meant to safeguard her sons, allowing them to keep their home. "That took a lot of courage," she said at last.

Ranger parked and stepped out of the car. "Yes, but she always had more than her share of that."

There were stones arranged in a circle around an outside campfire site, and he reached beneath one, bringing out a key that had been sealed inside a plastic sandwich bag. Ranger went over to the sturdy-looking door and used the key to unlock both brass locks.

Dana checked the door trim, but there was no circular design here like the one she'd seen on the other house near Farmington. If her suspicions were right and the marking indicated a Brotherhood of Warriors' or police safe house, this building wasn't included.

She followed him in, then, curious, studied the room carefully. The living area was sparsely furnished, with an old handmade wooden table constructed of pine planks, and several wooden chairs. The fireplace was big, made of stone, and looked like it could take off any chill on a cold evening. There was one simple wood-framed futon with a thick cushion in the center of the room. "That's modern," she said, surprised to see it there.

"The raccoons have a habit of breaking in and tearing up the furniture so we bought something that was comfortable and cheap."

"You and your brother?"

"Yes. We're twins."

Two men like Ranger? She couldn't even imagine it. "Are you identical?"

"Women always ask me that. Makes me wonder what they're thinking," he said, laughing. "But to answer your question, Hunter's my fraternal twin. There's a family resemblance, I suppose, but I don't think we look that much alike, nor do we act and think alike. But despite all that, we're close. I'll introduce you someday."

"I'd like that." Aware of how cold it was in the cabin, she rubbed her hands together for warmth and wished she'd brought a warmer jacket.

"I've got a better way of staying warm," he said, coming up from behind and wrapping his arms around her. "I guarantee results."

The promise swept over her like a slow, hot wind and her heart began thumping wildly. Taking a steadying breath, she forced her tone to stay cool and detached. "Of course you're talking about putting logs in the fireplace."

"Not really. That'll do the trick, too, I suppose, but it's not nearly as much fun," he added in her ear, then stepped away. "Make yourself at home. I'll go bring in some wood."

As he went through the small kitchen and out the back door, Dana breathed a sigh. The sparks between them practically made the air sizzle. The big difference was that, to her, those sparks were simply first steps down the path to something deeper. Yet, from what she'd learned about him, Ranger loved the sparks for their own sake.

She pushed back the thought. It was useless speculation. They had no future together. Soon, she'd be leaving him behind and setting out on her own to go find *Hastiin Díil*. She'd already come up with a plan. All she needed now was the chance to put it into motion.

Chapter Twelve

Dana sat alone on the hearth in front of a roaring fire. Nights in New Mexico could get very cold and tonight was no exception.

Ranger took a seat on the futon after placing more firewood on a cast-iron rack that looked homemade.

"I can't get that last evening with my friend out of my mind," she said quietly, staring into the fire. "If only I'd have seen what was going down sooner, or if I'd just reacted faster…."

"Stop. That's exactly what you should *not* do. Second-guessing yourself is only going to make you crazy. Believe me."

It was the way his voice dropped when he'd spoken those last two words that instantly captured her attention. "You have your own nightmares to deal with, don't you?" she asked in a whisper, her heart going out to him. No matter what else was in play, they'd both lost someone who mattered to them.

He nodded. "That's one of the reasons I chose

to come here. This cabin, to me, is a place of healing," he said, then added, "grab your jacket. There's something I'd like you to see."

Once outside, it took a few minutes for her eyes to adjust to the darkness, but the moonlight was bright. He led her to the side of the fence that bordered the back and pointed to a small climbing vine.

"In the sunlight the leaves of that plant are a bright blue-green," he began in a quiet voice. "It was my mother's favorite plant. The vine isn't supposed to grow at this altitude, but my mother kept bringing seeds and cuttings and wouldn't give up. Then one day the vine began to grow. It's been there for the last twenty or so years. It dies back after the first frost of the season then returns every spring covered with small orange flowers," he said, then in a thoughtful voice added, "that vine is my mother's way of reminding us that time, and love, can work miracles, and love endures, no matter how difficult its beginning."

Ranger pulled her into his arms and for a moment held her gaze. His dark eyes gleamed with desire…and something more. Knowledge? For that one instant she was almost sure that he'd guessed she was planning to escape. But that was impossible…wasn't it?

When his lips covered hers, all her thoughts faded away. The pounding of his heart against hers, the roughness and possessiveness of his kiss, bathed her in exquisite sensations.

By the time he eased his hold, her knees were ready to buckle. She shivered, holding onto him out of necessity as well as desire.

"Let's go back inside," he said.

She nodded. If only they'd met under different circumstances. Ranger's courage and his determination to restore harmony and balance said more about him than words ever could. Now, to complete what she had to do, she'd have to find the same qualities in herself. She'd given her word to *Hastiin Sani,* and it was time to honor that commitment.

She pulled her hand away from his as they reached the hearth. "I guess I'm more tired than I thought," she said. "I'm going to call it a night."

As she went down the hall, she palmed the car keys from the table then stepped into the bedroom. Pulling the door half-shut, she blew out the kerosene lamp. Then she waited, sitting in the dark and listening. She wouldn't try the window until she was sure he'd gone to sleep.

She already had a plan. She'd let the car roll downhill as far as possible before starting it up. That promised to be the tricky part—hoping the noise wouldn't wake him. If she was lucky, she'd be able to get a good head start and he'd never catch up.

Minutes slipped by with agonizing slowness.

She could hear him moving around in the living room. Finally, when it was close to four in the morning, she couldn't hear him anymore.

Dana crept to the double hung window, unfastened the lever at the top and pulled the bottom half up slowly. On closer inspection, it was even narrower than she'd thought. No matter how much she pushed and maneuvered trying to get her shoulders through, there wasn't enough clearance. She then tried feet first, and got as far as her ribs, but no farther.

Bruised but unhurt, Dana closed the window, fastened the latch, then returned to the bed, frustrated. She'd never make it out either door, not with him in the living room. Of that she was certain.

Moments after she'd returned to the bed, he knocked softly at the door. "You all right?"

"What?" she managed in a muffled voice.

"Sorry. Didn't mean to wake you. Just wanted to make sure everything's all right. Thought I heard something, then I felt a draft." He came into the room and checked the window.

She watched him, glad now that she'd shut and latched it. "Could you open it a crack? I know it's cold, but I really like a little fresh air at night."

He smiled and pushed it up about four inches. "Too much?"

"No, just right. You can close the door completely if you think I'm going to freeze you to death."

"I've got plenty of blankets, and the warmth of the fireplace." He lingered at her door for a second.

"Something wrong?" she asked.

He shook his head. "Sleep well."

As soon as he left, she breathed a sigh of relief. It was time for a new plan. She'd wait till morning and see what kind of situation presented itself then. The first chance she got, she'd be gone.

SHORTLY AFTER SUNRISE, Ranger left the cabin, then facing east, took a pinch of pollen from his *jish* and made an offering to the Holy Ones, asking for protection and blessings.

Once his morning ritual ended, he walked back into the cabin. Last night he'd heard Dana open the window, then shut it. He had a feeling that she'd planned to make a run for it, but discovered that the windows were just too small to climb through. He already knew she'd taken the keys from the table. Everything was going according to plan.

He'd give her a chance to escape today and see what she did. The last time he'd spoken to his brother, he'd told Hunter that he believed Dana could be trusted. But Hunter had required proof, and had come up with a plan to test her. Ranger had been ordered to give Dana a chance to slip away, then follow her. If she went to Trujillo or one of his henchmen to report, they'd have their answer.

Ranger had brought her here to where there'd be an extra set of wheels waiting. Regardless of which vehicle Dana stole, he'd be able to pursue. He kept an extra key to both vehicles with him at all times, and the truck and the sedan had hidden GPS devices so they could be tracked.

As he stepped into the kitchen, Dana turned her head and smiled at him. "Good morning. Is there anything to eat here?" she asked, rummaging through the cupboards.

"There's cereal and powdered milk in the top shelf," he said, pointing.

She turned to look, and he took a quick glance at the hall table. The keys were there.

"Found it," she said. "Do you want some, too?"

He shook his head. "I'll eat later. I just wanted to let you know I'll be outside for about twenty minutes. I'm going to reconnoiter the area."

"You're going to do what?"

"I need to make sure no one's picked up our trail, so I'm hiking farther up the mountain to a good observation spot. By the time you finish breakfast, I should be back. If you need me, just come up the trail beyond the woodpile."

Ranger went out the back door, wearing his shoulder holster and .45 pistol beneath his jacket. Now it began.

He continued past the woodpile, then climbed

about fifty yards farther into the forest. From this spot, surrounded by vegetation and hidden in the shade, he had a good view of both vehicles. All he had to do now was wait.

After several minutes Dana came out and headed for the truck, keys in hand. For a moment he thought that she hadn't realized that the keys were for the car. Then he saw her bend down by the truck tire.

Dana reached down, but then shook her head, and walked quickly to the sedan. Apparently, she'd thought about flattening the tire, then changed her mind, not wanting to leave him stranded. In a backward sort of way, his respect for her went up a notch. Her actions meant she believed in doing the right thing—which also meant she couldn't be associated with Trujillo.

Ranger watched as Dana climbed into the sedan, released the brake, then steered as it rolled down the lane, making almost no noise at all except for the tires crunching on the gravel. The car was already out of sight around the first curve when she finally started the engine.

He dialed his brother on the cell phone while jogging back down the trail to the truck. "She took the car," Ranger said. "For the record, she thought about disabling the truck, but changed her mind."

"If you need backup, call in. I'll have a few men I can trust close by."

"You're wrong about her, brother," Ranger said. "I think I know where she's going. It took me awhile to put things together, but there's only one answer that makes sense. The medicine man knew about her photographic memory and found a way to make use of it. If I'm right, she's going to try to find *Hastiin Díil* to give him names. She hasn't said anything about her plans because she was undoubtedly sworn to secrecy."

"Do you think she has any idea where to go find him?" Hunter asked.

"Maybe. I suspected that she'd used the computer at the safe house so I searched its memory. I know she did an Internet search on medicine men and medicine hogans. It's possible she also read a news article lifted from the tribal newspaper and has figured out the location of *Hastiin Díil*'s medicine hogan. That's no secret, because our new leader is also a well-known healer."

"You're making a dangerous assumption—that she's innocent, and had nothing to do with the death of the Singer. But based on what?"

"I trust my instincts," Ranger said, climbing into the truck and starting the engine.

"You said you believed she has the names of the Brotherhood of Warriors. If so, then she must know that you're part of us."

"The way I see it, she didn't get all the names

because I don't think she knows quite what to make of me. I would have seen some kind of indication if she knew I was in the brotherhood. But it's also possible she's guarding the secret she was given."

"So we'll play this out and see what we get," Hunter said. "Trujillo's place—or more to the point, one of his places—is southeast of Farmington, near the Bolack Ranch. There's only one road leading from the highway, so if she goes in that direction, you'll have your answer. But what if she decides to make a phone call instead? There are pay phones at every convenience store between Shiprock and that location."

"Then she only has to go as far as Shiprock, doesn't she?" Ranger answered. "I'll stay close in case she makes a stop, and keep in touch." As Ranger ended the call, he took out the small unit with the GPS screen and turned it on. It would show, on a simple display, where Dana was headed.

He'd been certain that she wouldn't go to Trujillo's, and was satisfied to see that his guess had been right. Currently she was taking the road that led to a small community called Rattlesnake. It was a mixed area, but traditionalists outnumbered modern Navajos four to one.

Ranger dialed his brother as he hurried on, taking a shortcut down a fire road that would get him out of the foothills. "Are there any medicine hogans close to Rattlesnake? She's driving south in that direction."

Hunter didn't respond right away. "Not that I recall, but there's the *Bilagáana* Trading Post. It's farther south down the same road, maybe ten miles from Rattlesnake."

Ranger had heard of it. *Bilagáana* meant *white man,* and the trading post had been aptly named by the white man who ran it. Jonas Sullivan was in his eighties, and had lived among the *Diné* almost all of his adult life. Jonas was one of the few white men who truly understood the concept of the *Hohzo*— maintaining beauty, order, harmony and stability in one's life. Though it was a concept the Anglo world—the white world—found unattainable for the most part, Jonas Sullivan walked in beauty.

Twenty-five minutes later, after having just topped the hill leading into Rattlesnake, he saw the sedan passing the last house of the old settlement. Hanging back, he followed the dust trail down the graveled road.

Dana reached the trading post, a low, white cinder block structure with a nearly flat metal roof and one of those old-west-style fronts. She parked and walked right past the pay phone, disappearing into the store.

Ranger parked just down the road beside a small grove of stunted trees and waited. She was on a hunt of her own, but it wasn't for a phone, obviously, or Trujillo, unless she was meeting him there. But that seemed unlikely. Trujillo, like Dana, would be remembered by everyone who saw him.

Ranger leaned back and prepared to wait and see how things played out.

DANA WENT INSIDE the trading post, stepping around the familiar potbelly stove, well-stoked at the moment to take the chill out of the interior. A cast-iron kettle on the top was steaming, adding humidity to the dry desert air.

Although it was barely 9:00 a.m., the general store was already crowded. Most of the patrons were Navajos, but there were two or three adventurous Anglo tourists who'd taken the back roads early today.

The sights and scents were all familiar to her— canned and packaged food, saddles, leather goods, garden implements and motor oil. Space in establishments like these was always at a premium, and every counter, corner and section of wall was lined with merchandise.

Soon Dana spotted Jonas Sullivan, the owner, speaking to a Navajo woman holding a child. Although he'd glanced her way, he hadn't recognized her. She hadn't seen him in over a decade but, to her, he hadn't changed much. As far back as she could remember, Mr. Sullivan had always appeared old to her.

She waited, looking at some finely woven Navajo rugs. Most had the natural blacks, whites and browns of undyed wools. Woven from handspun wool, these were exquisite, and expensive as well. Mr. Sullivan had always carried the best of the best—including her mother's paintings of the Navajo Nation. Dana waited her turn patiently, and eventually he came over.

"May I help you, ma'am?" he asked.

Dana beamed him her best smile. "Mr. Sullivan, don't you remember me?"

His eyes narrowed and suddenly he smiled. "Dana! Of course! I haven't seen you in ages. You know, I still have one of your mother's paintings of Window Rock hanging in my living room."

He lowered his voice, looking around cautiously. "I heard on the news that you had been the victim of a crime, and were now a protected witness."

"I am," she answered softly. "Is there someplace we can talk privately?"

"Follow me." He took her behind the counter, nodding to the young Navajo clerk as they passed by.

Jonas had always lived in the back of his trading post, and as they stepped into his living room, she noticed that the interior was even more crowded than she'd remembered.

"What brings you all the way out here? Do you need my help?" he asked, waving her to the faded green couch.

"I need some information," she said, sitting down. The cushions were so worn, she practically sank into them. "I came to you because you've lived in this area since before I was born. You must know just about everyone."

He laughed. "I don't know about that, but tell me what you need."

"I have to find a medicine man—at least I *think* he's a medicine man. But whatever it is he does, I'm betting he's well-respected by the tribe. He goes by the name of *Hastiin Dííl*," she said, careful not to reveal anything more than was absolutely necessary.

Jonas nodded. "I know who you're talking about, but finding him won't be easy. He lives northwest of here, almost to Beclabito. But you have to go in from the south because of the road. It's not much more than a dirt track."

"If he's close to Beclabito, he might have electricity and a phone," she said, thinking out loud.

"I don't think so. And I should warn you—no one seems to know where he is at the moment. I've had several people stop by and ask me about him."

"Patients?"

"Yes, and friends, too. The most recent was an Anglo man. He was the one in the T-shirt and baggy pants who was at the magazine rack when you came in. The guy in the baseball cap," he added.

Remembering what Jenny had told her about a man wearing a cap, she followed up instantly. "I noticed him, but I thought he was just another tourist. A man in his thirties, right? Do you remember what the writing on the front of his shirt said, maybe the name of a company or school?"

"No, it was something like Gone to the Dogs. He smelled funny, too, come to think of it, like a wet dog," he added with a smirk. "Maybe he owns a kennel."

"Did you tell him where the hogan was?" she asked.

"No, I said I didn't know. There was something…off…about him and I trust my instincts. But I noticed that he spoke to some of the other customers, so it's possible someone else gave him that information."

She got directions to *Hastiin Dííl*'s medicine hogan, then stood up and thanked Jonas.

"Dana, you be careful out there," he said. "I know you're in the thick of things right now, and from what I heard on the news, you have some bad people looking for you."

"One of those bad people might be the guy in the baseball cap. If he's still hanging around, will you try to delay him?"

"You bet I will."

When they returned to the store area, the man in the cap was no longer in the building. Dana hurried out to the sedan and was soon on her way. As she pushed the car along the pothole ridden road, the Carrizo Mountains ahead and just to the west, she began to wish that she'd taken Ranger's truck instead. The sedan might have been able to do one hundred on the highway without a problem, but on this type of road, she needed the suspension system of a truck. The car bounced along in protest, sounding as if it were ready to fall apart any second.

As she came out of an arroyo, Dana caught a glimpse of a plume of dust rising high into the air behind her. Someone *was* following her. Maybe the man in the cap had spotted her, waited within sight of the parking lot, then gone after her once she'd left.

Despite the danger, there was one bright spot. If the guy had managed to get *Hastiin Dííl*'s location, he wouldn't have been following her now. He would have taken the lead.

There was no way she was going to lead him to the Singer, so she pulled off the road where it crossed a shallow arroyo, then drove down the center to a spot where it curved. Slowing down to a crawl, then coming to a stop, she turned off the engine, got out of the car and waited where she could see the road from behind cover.

Soon, a brand-new, red pickup roared past, traveling at a fast clip. Though it was a test of her patience, she returned to the car, climbed inside, then remained stationary for another twenty minutes, listening. Nobody came back from the direction she was heading, so the red truck had continued on.

Finally, not willing to wait any longer, she drove back out to the road, grateful she hadn't gotten stuck in the soft sand. This terrain was difficult and, since she'd been without a cell phone, she would have had no way of calling for help if she'd become stranded.

Watching the ground ahead anxiously, Dana flinched when she heard a loud bang, like a gunshot. Almost simultaneously she heard a loud pop just to her left, followed by a whoosh just outside. The steering wheel nearly jerked out of her grip as the car abruptly pulled to the left.

Her left front tire had obviously gone flat and it was no accident. Stopping now would be suicide. She was under attack. Struggling to maintain control, Dana let off the gas, fighting the impulse to hit the brakes as the vehicle slid downhill at an angle. She couldn't afford to roll the car.

Glancing in her side mirror, she saw a man running after the car, rifle in hand. Another one carrying a pistol was coming from her left, running to intercept her car. She stepped on the gas pedal and the engine roared but the car just fishtailed. There was no way to pick up speed on this terrain with a flat.

It was time to bail. Dana swerved hard to her right, hit the brakes and jumped out. She raced up the canyon, hoping the car would block her from any more gunfire. All she had to do was make it around the curve in the big wash. Hearing the distinct whine of a bullet passing overhead, she ducked and ran even faster.

Chapter Thirteen

Dana tried her best to stay on hard ground and not leave a trail as she searched for a place to hide. She wasn't armed and although she could defend herself, her chances against two armed men weren't good.

The only thing working in her favor was that they clearly wanted her alive. Otherwise, they would have both blasted away at the car when she slowed down to enter the arroyo. They wouldn't have aimed for the tire, either.

That gave her some hope. Trujillo undoubtedly knew about her photographic memory, and the attack meant he was pulling out all the stops to get her back and force her to tell whatever she remembered. Of course after they were finished, they'd kill her, just like they had *Hastiin Sani*.

Dana kept moving—slowly, and in a crouch—and stayed in the shadows offered by the nearly vertical fifteen-foot-high sides of the wash. Her chances were slim, especially if she was forced into a sandy part of the arroyo that would show her tracks, but she refused to give up. She stood still and listened. Less than a hundred feet away was the man with the pistol searching for her footprints on the hard ground, and the one with the rifle was at the top rim of the arroyo, watching with binoculars.

Before she could decide what to do, Dana felt a stirring in the air and, out of the corner of her eye, saw a fleeting shadow. Suddenly Ranger stepped out of a narrow crevice in the arroyo, less than three feet away.

Her heart was hammering frantically but before she could say a word, he placed a finger to his lips. He indicated with a thumb the approximate location of the two men, then gestured ahead to the center of the arroyo. It was piled high with wind-blown tumbleweeds the size of washing machines.

Ranger moved into the bramble and Dana followed. It had seemed impassable but, somehow, Ranger found a pathway through the thicket.

They made headway quicker than she'd thought possible, circling and ducking beneath the sticky barrier. She could hear the men behind them, feeling their way along, cursing constantly, but still closing in. Her heart pounding, she looked ahead for Ranger's truck, but it was impossible to see any farther than ten feet ahead.

"Through there," he said and pointed.

They reached the truck moments later. He'd parked in a wide, shallow part of the arroyo, near where the road paralleled the wash. Ranger dove behind the steering wheel as she climbed in and fastened her belt. In a heartbeat they were on the move.

She kept her eyes on the road behind them, but no one pursued. "I don't understand. Why did you come after me after I took off? You don't even trust me, yet you risked your life for mine again."

He paused for a moment before answering her, searching for the right words. "You've been holding out on me," he said at last. "I've known that all along. But I still trust my instincts about you."

Tears of frustration stung her eyes. No matter how much she wanted to, she couldn't tell him what she knew. Her dying friend had trusted her with his biggest secret and she wouldn't let him down.

"How did you find me?" she asked at last, her voice as unsteady as she felt.

"I was ordered to give you a chance to run away. I've been tracking you for hours. I didn't know where you'd go, but I was sure it wouldn't be to Trujillo," he said. "And I know you didn't stop to call him, either."

"*Who* ordered you?" she pressed.

"I can't tell you. In fact, I've probably said too much already."

She nodded slowly, understanding. From everything she knew about him, he was a man of honor. She had a feeling that Ranger's name had been on the portion of the list she hadn't seen. But there was no way for her to know for sure. If Ranger really was a part of the Brotherhood of Warriors and she asked him outright, he'd deny it. He had his own loyalties and oaths to honor, too.

"Trujillo wants me—and it's not because I'm his friend," she said at last.

"I know."

When they reached the crest of the tallest mesa around, Ranger reversed directions and parked where they could see for miles in every direction.

"Let's see if we can spot where they're headed. Hand me the binoculars from the glove compartment," he asked.

By the time he had the binoculars, all he could see was a tail of dust fading away in the distance. "I was hoping they'd follow us, and we could set our own trap, or follow them," he said. "But they've gone in the opposite direction. We'll never catch up to them now."

Ranger shifted in his seat and faced her. "But there's one point I want to make right now. If they'd captured you, you would have been forced to give up whatever information you carry. Then they would have killed you, and by then, it would have been a mercy. I want you to be very aware of what you're up against—and why you need me."

She'd already come to that conclusion, but hearing it out loud made her start trembling. Dana clasped her hands together and took a deep breath, willing herself to stop. "I know all that, but there's nothing I can do right now to change the situation. The most I can tell you is that there are things I have to do by myself."

"Like finding *Hastiin Díil?*"

"Jonas *told* you?"

"He trusts me more than you do. And he also knows me very well and realizes the information is safe with me."

"I gave my word to a man who meant the world to me—your tribe's medicine man," she said, fighting the tears stinging her eyes. "I've *got* to find *Hastiin Díil.*"

He shook his head. "Can't be done, at least not right now. Too many bad guys are trying to find him, too, so he's gone underground. But if you've got something important to say to him, tell me, and I'll do my best to see he gets the message."

They were at an impasse, but she needed help to finish what she'd promised *Hastiin Sani* she'd do. Dana closed her eyes for a second, searching her heart for the answer.

A moment later she opened her eyes and met his

gaze. Her instincts about Ranger couldn't be that off the mark. Everything she'd seen assured her he could be trusted.

Making her decision, she took a deep breath. "The kidnappers forced the medicine man to give them a list of names. *Hastiin Dííl*'s was the first one written down. Maybe that's why the killers remembered and passed it on to Trujillo."

"Did you see the list?" he pressed.

"You know about loyalty and about honoring your word. You should understand why I can't tell you anything more."

"Trujillo and his people want *Hastiin Dííl* because they remember his name. But they also want you because they're assuming you know the other names. The list must have been lost at some point, so your photographic memory is the only record they can access. Am I close?" he asked.

"They're overestimating my worth," she said, then held up her hand and shook her head. "That's all I can say."

Ranger considered her words for a long time. "Trujillo's men won't go back to *Hastiin Dííl*'s hogan. There were two vehicles following you before, and one of them went in another direction after leaving the trading post. If I'm right, *those* goons went directly to his hogan. By now they've had time to break in, search the place and leave.

They wouldn't have had any reason to stick around, because the medicine man isn't there. Why don't you and I go over to *Hastiin Dííl*'s place and see if we can pick up a clue that'll lead us to him?"

"So you don't know where he is, either?"

"No, and no one's going to give me that information based on what I have so far," he said.

Ranger was risking all that he held dear for her. "Thank you for trusting me."

"We're part of something bigger, you and I. That means rules have to be broken." He picked up his cell phone, checked and realized he had service. "This is Wind," he said identifying himself in a way that would tell his brother he wasn't alone. "I'm going to *Hastiin Dííl*'s hogan."

"He's not there. You know that," Hunter answered. "No one can reach him where he is now. He's safe."

"Can you?"

There was a pause. "No. I don't have that information."

And that was what he'd wanted to know. "I'll be in touch."

"You still haven't told me why—"

"Later."

She looked at him. "Is Wind your nickname?"

"I use it in business. It's a name that seems to fit me."

She nodded in agreement. He could be fierce or as gentle as a breeze in summer. He could move in total silence and leave no evidence of his passing. Wind was the perfect code name for him.

Despite knowing the red truck had gone in the opposite direction, Ranger was very cautious, stopping often to make sure no one was on his tail.

Satisfied after a long circuitous route, they finally drove to *Hastiin Dííl's*. Two log hogans, their joints sealed with clay, were side by side, but one was considerably larger than the other. From what she'd read, Dana knew that the larger hogan with the smoke hole and the blanket over the doorway was the medicine hogan.

"Don't," he said, as she started to open the door. "I'm not even going to turn the engine off. Let's wait a bit and make sure we're not getting suckered into a trap. They could be on foot, inside."

Parked behind a cluster of trees, he left the engine idling. They waited for over ten minutes before he finally pulled the key out. "Keep your eyes open and stay sharp," he said, his gaze never resting.

"This place looks completely deserted," she said, looking around as she opened the passenger's door.

"Don't trust anything. Expect the unexpected and it won't broadside you."

He walked over, then crouched down by a set of vehicle tracks. "A large pickup was here," he said.

"Probably *Hastiin Dííl*'s, don't you think?"

"No, here are his vehicle's tracks. He drives a VW bus. It's ancient, but he loves it. His tracks are a few days old, considering the amount of dust that settled over them," he said.

"These others, the ones from the pickup, must be fairly new then," she said, taking a closer look.

"We have no proof that the truck belonged to Trujillo's men, but I'm almost certain it did. Those are brand-new tires, and it's a six-wheeled pickup. Most of our people can't afford the fancy stuff." He stood. "Stay put. I'm going to take a look at the residence."

"Do you have a key?" she asked.

"Traditionalists don't generally lock doors," he said, then added, "But all things considered, he may have decided to start. I'll find out soon enough."

He strode off to the hogan being used as a home—the one with the stovepipe passing through the center of the roof and the solid wooden door.

Dana watched him go around to the front. Finding the door partially open, he stuck his head inside. While he was busy with that, she kept watch for trouble. A cottontail rushing about caught her eye and, as she watched him scamper off, she spotted a set of footprints.

Following them, she realized they came from the arroyo and led almost directly to the medicine hogan. From the absence of windblown dust over them, she could tell the visitor had been there today. She followed the tracks to the medicine hogan, then, looking up, saw Ranger walking in her direction.

"I found some footprints, so I'm going to take a quick look," she called out to him. Since women also had Sings done, she knew she wouldn't be violating any taboos by peering inside. She drew the blanket aside about a foot, then stuck her head inside.

A click followed by a thud caught her attention immediately and a roundish object rolled by her boot. Ranger leaped forward, scooped it up, then hurled it toward the arroyo. Spinning around, he knocked her down, and covered her with his body.

The ground shook from a deafening blast and the air was alive with screeching, flying debris. She heard thumps all along the log sides of the hogan. Hearing a thud to her right, she shifted her gaze and saw a jagged, foot-long splinter of wood jammed into the ground inches from Ranger's head.

He kept her pinned for several more seconds as debris continued to rain down, then finally rolled clear. A cloud of dust was starting to settle around them. "From now on, I go in first. To heck with the Anglo ladies' first custom."

She was shaking so hard her teeth were chattering as he helped her to her feet. "Are you hurt?" he asked, looking her over.

She looked down at herself, unable to even mutter a simple yes-or-no answer. Now that it was over, the reality of what had just happened slammed into her with a vengeance. Tears stung her eyes, and she couldn't stop shaking.

He pulled her into his arms and she didn't resist. The gentleness of his embrace gave her an anchor and a haven in the midst of the violence that surrounded them. "That wooden spike could have killed you."

Before he could answer, she drew his mouth down to hers. A verbal thank-you for all he'd done would have never been enough to convey what she was feeling. She needed to show him what was in her heart. She wanted him to feel what she did, that crazy swirl of gentle emotions edged with fire.

Dana pressed herself into the kiss, tasting him tentatively, then more boldly. His welcoming tenderness made everything inside her melt. Flickers of delicious pleasure that started at the pit of her stomach and wound downward ignited a more desperate need, and she felt herself drowning in its intensity.

With a deep groan, Ranger eased his hold. "We can't, not now. We have to get going, and I've got to let others know what happened here." Ranger turned to look at the heavily damaged medicine hogan. "I'm going to find the lowlife who did this. Count on it."

When Ranger looked back at her, Dana saw that his earlier gentleness had vanished and been replaced by a ruthlessness she'd never dreamed he possessed.

"A quick death here and now would have been more merciful than what they have planned for me," she said in a barely audible voice.

He pressed his palm to her cheek, forcing her to look at him. "You may walk away from me freely someday, but I'll die before I let anyone take you. I *will* keep you safe." He held her gaze for a brief eternity.

When he turned away at long last, his gaze traveled to what was left of the hogan. The blast had driven several of the logs inward, dislodging them from their notched joints like sticks. The roof had given way above, and now sagged almost within arm's reach in places.

"We need to call the tribal police," she said.

"We will, but give me a moment."

He crouched and began to study the splinters of wood and chunks of hardened clay now scattered around the partially collapsed entrance.

Dana joined him. "Let me help," she said. "What are we looking for?"

"The pin and the handle from the grenade. They should still be around here somewhere. But *look,* don't *touch.* The FBI will have to go through all of this with a fine-tooth comb and the less we disturb the scene, the more thorough their job can be. All I'm trying to do is figure out how new their ordinance is."

As she began searching through the rubble, the reality of how close Ranger had come to death hit her hard. He could have just dove to the ground, yet he'd chosen to grab the explosive, throw it away, then shield her with his own body. That knowledge impacted on every part of her being. At one point she'd wondered if he really cared about her. She had no doubts now. There was no greater proof of love.

When she stepped back to get an overview, she saw the blood on the back of Ranger's shirt and pants leg. For a second her heart forgot to beat. Then, as pure instinct took over, she ran to his side. "You're hurt. You need help."

Chapter Fourteen

Seeing the look on her face, Ranger brushed his knuckles against her cheek. "Stop worrying. I can handle it. They're just minor cuts—shrapnel or flying debris."

"You need a doctor."

Ranger shook his head. "It'll have to wait. I want to identify the ordinance first. Then I've got to make sure *Hastiin Dííl*'s hogan isn't wired, too."

"Another grenade?" she said in a thin voice.

"Or a bomb," he said, then spotting something of interest to him, took a few steps away. Using the tip of his boot, he brushed aside some debris, and found a metal handle. "It's U.S. Vietnam-era ordinance. Old, but still deadly."

"How would anyone get something like that?"

"Ignacio's brother was an army veteran from that conflict," Ranger said. "It was probably a souvenir he carried or mailed home to himself."

Favoring his right leg, Ranger walked from the

damaged medicine hogan to *Hastiin Dííl*'s home, which had sustained no visible damage from the blast. Even the small window in the door and the bigger window halfway around the small hexagonal building were still intact.

"What if you find a bomb? You're not going to try to disable it, are you?" she asked, her voice rising another octave.

"That'll depend on how it's set up. Whoever did this meant to kill *Hastiin Dííl*. He obviously won't be returning anytime soon, but others could be in danger. A neighbor or one of his patients might come by, decide to leave a note or something, and get killed. If I can disable the triggering device then we can go but, if not, we'll have to stick around until the police arrive."

He was right. As dangerous as it was to stay in one place for long, they couldn't just leave. "Okay, then it's settled. Tell me how I can help."

He gave her an approving nod. "Don't touch *anything,* but look around the walls, window and ground for trip wires, string, batteries, springs, pieces of pipe, even a clothespin—anything unusual or out of place. Move slow, making sure you're not stepping on anything but undisturbed ground, and don't lean against any part of the structure, especially anything that might move together or apart."

"Got it," she said.

Dana began her search, walking slowly toward the side window, while he stepped over to the hogan door. As he bent to check around the door handle with a penlight, she heard his gut-wrenching groan. It was the raw sound of pure pain.

She went to his side. "You've got several wounds on your back. If you won't go to a doctor or hospital, at least let me take a look and see how bad they are," she said. "Teachers are required to take a first-aid course."

"It'll wait. I'm in no danger of dying. Just be my extra set of eyes over here around the door," he said, bringing her focus back to the business at hand. "We'll take care of the cuts later."

She peered into the single pane of glass set into the door. "Can I borrow your penlight for a second?" She looked down, aiming the light. "There's some string attached to the inside handle leading to a clothespin. It's connected to a sliver of wood by the jaws. I also see what look like wires around the clothespin. And there's something in aluminum foil on the floor, just behind the door."

"All right, back away," he said. "Clothespins are common makeshift triggers. When whatever is holding the jaws apart gets pulled out, the jaws close and connect two strips of foil or wire. That completes a circuit that sets off the device."

"Leave the disarming job to someone else," she insisted. "You're hurt and you won't be able to concentrate, not totally anyway, and the only way you can get to it is by climbing in through the window. You won't be able to do that. You're in pain. I can see it on your face."

"We don't have the tools we need anyway. Looks like we'll have to stay here."

"Do you have a first-aid kit in your truck?" she asked.

He nodded. "Beneath the seat on the passenger side."

They walked over to his truck, Dana helping him. Along the way, he called in a report on his cell phone.

"I'm all yours," he said, ending the call and folding up the phone. "Are you sure you can handle this?"

"I won't know until I have a look. Let me help you take your shirt off and we'll start with your back."

As she stood in front of him, unbuttoning his shirt, she could feel his breath brush her skin like a light caress. "If it's bad, you *will* have to go to a clinic or hospital."

"It's not that bad. I'd know if it was."

She slipped the shirt off his shoulders carefully. "Turn around," she said, trying to keep her voice steady.

A moment later she found three shallow cuts, probably from metal or slivers of wood or rocks that had been sent flying at high speed. But there didn't appear to be any foreign material in the wounds. "I can clean and disinfect these. But there's still the back of your thigh. There's a lot more blood on your pant leg, and I think you're still bleeding down there."

"Yeah, I can feel it," he agreed.

"Drop your jeans," she said, after finishing with his back. "I need to take a look."

"Remember, you asked," he said.

Before she could decide if he'd issued a challenge or was just teasing, he unbuckled his belt and lowered his pants. He was wearing no underwear.

"*Don't* turn around," she said breathlessly.

His chuckle was more like a deep-throated growl, and it made a skin-prickling warmth spread through her.

She swore to herself that she'd remain professional and wouldn't look at anything but the back of his thigh. But she wasn't made of stone. Her gaze rose upward slightly and she saw what could only be described as world-class buns. Yearning and a hot blast of desire spiraled around her. Ranger was temptation itself.

"So how deep is it?"

She took an unsteady breath and focused. "There's a sliver of metal about the size of a dime imbedded in your skin. It needs to come out. After that, I'll need to clean and disinfect the wound thoroughly, but it's going to bleed even more then, at least for a while. The alcohol's going to sting."

"I can handle it…can you?" he asked in a whisper-soft voice.

"Handle… Yes, of course," she said, disciplining her thoughts.

She worked quickly, using small forceps from the kit to pull out the piece of shrapnel, then applying pressure to stem the bleeding before disinfecting the area. For a brief second or two as she bandaged his wound, wayward thoughts filled her mind. It would have been so easy to leave a string of kisses down his back and force both of them to forget everything else. She sighed.

"Someday…" he whispered as if reading her mind.

That one word, so rich with promise, touched her aching soul. She wanted him, and the feeling was more powerful than anything she'd ever experienced. It wasn't wise, wasn't logical, wasn't orderly, and yet it was as real as the wind that rose from the west and swept through the canyon.

"I've done all I can for now," she said, more assured now that the bleeding had stopped. She thought back to the way her life had been once—punctuated by plans and orderly schedules. Yet, in retrospect, it just seemed empty somehow.

As he pulled up his jeans, he turned around,

letting her see him for a moment or two. Her breath stuck in her throat as she saw how aroused…and how big…he was.

"Today's not ours," he whispered, "but someday soon…" He brushed a light kiss on her forehead. "Hand me my shirt, then help me keep watch."

TIME PASSED SLOWLY. He wanted her, but his wasn't the kind of need that would be satisfied after a few hours of passion. His feelings for Dana went much deeper…and that was what would eventually break both their hearts.

They were just too different. He lived life in the present, never knowing what the next day would bring. He thrived on the danger and the uncertainty that came with his profession. Dana needed order, security and a routine.

Ranger stole a glance at her and forced himself to look at things the way they really were. Secrets still stood between them, though perhaps they weren't quite so secret anymore. But where even one secret existed, others found fertile ground. The only closeness they'd ever know totally would be a physical one.

They'd have their day. That was inevitable. And it would be an experience neither of them would ever forget. There'd be no regrets—but there would be heartache, sooner or later.

"Someone's coming," Dana said.

He listened for a second, then nodded. "We'll keep watch from the truck in case we have to make a fast getaway. Let's go," he said. A moment later she was buckling her seat belt while he sat behind the wheel.

A call came in on his cell phone and Ranger picked it up. The caller quickly identified himself as the tribal police officer, now approaching the scene in his patrol unit.

"I was told to make sure I let you know when I got close," the officer said. "Agent Harris said he would speak to you later."

Ranger nodded, seeing the tribal unit now, a quarter mile away. The brotherhood was making itself felt. Otherwise Harris would have been more of a problem. His brother had undoubtedly called in a few markers.

As they left the area, Ranger made two quick calls. The first was to his brother, updating him in a short staccato burst, and then to Tony Birdsong, asking him to pick up the sedan from where he'd left it.

"Things just keep getting worse, don't they?" Dana said softly. "For all practical purposes I've got a bull's eye on my back, and you're fair game because you're with me."

He didn't answer. The truth was he was also in danger because he was part of the brotherhood.

When his cell phone rang again, Ranger flipped it open. Hunter's voice came through clearly.

"Here's what I've got for you. The big pickup used to run you two off the road yesterday is being processed by the FBI. It was stolen, so they'll have to rely on fingerprints and whatever other physical evidence they turn up. Tribal officers are questioning the people at the trading post who saw the Anglo man who ambushed Dana. Jonas gave them a description, too, but his sight isn't what it used to be, and his clerk didn't give the man more than a passing glance because he was with other customers. There were no security cameras."

"There's no telling who's on Trujillo's hit list," Ranger said. "Watch your back."

"I hope they do come after me. I've got some backup in place. They'll get one heckuva fight," Hunter said then added, "stay sharp out there."

"Don't worry. Like the wind, we'll slip right through their grasp." Hearing his brother's chuckle, Ranger ended the call.

"We need a base of operations—somewhere they can't track us," Ranger said.

"Agreed. But where?"

"I'm going to take you to my place. It's not registered under my name for a reason—when I don't want to be found, I'm not."

"Nobody knows where you live?" she asked incredulously.

"I have two places. One's near town and pretty much public knowledge. The other, the one I'm talking about, is my getaway—the one I go to when I need time to myself."

"Then let's go. I'm tired of running. Everywhere we go, we run into my enemies."

"Your enemies are also mine."

She gave him a gentle smile. "I really wish that weren't the case."

"You want to protect *me?*"

She nodded. "And why not?"

He felt an answering tug deep inside himself, but pushed it aside immediately. To guard her effectively, he'd have to stay on track.

"When we get to my place, I'll contact some people I know, and find out if the police have any leads they haven't shared with us. I'll also do my best to find out where Trujillo is most vulnerable. A good offense will be our best defense."

"Sounds like you've already got an idea," she said.

"Yeah, I do, but I still need to work a few things out."

Chapter Fifteen

His getaway turned out to be a simple wood-frame farmhouse on the north bank of the San Juan River west of Shiprock. The home was a rectangle of wood siding and fiberglass shingles, a style that could have easily been found in Utah or California instead of the Navajo Nation.

As they stepped up onto the wooden porch Dana noticed the same circular symbol carved into the door frame that she'd seen at the first house they'd stayed. It was scarcely more than a scratch in the wood near the floorboard, but it was there.

Unlocking his door, Ranger turned and, following her gaze, saw what she'd been studying. "I have some creative termites," he said with a half smile. "Pesky creatures."

She said nothing, but her thoughts were racing. It didn't seem likely that Ranger's home was a police safe house. It made more sense to believe Ranger was a member of the Brotherhood of

Warriors and this was a symbol another member in trouble would recognize.

From what she'd seen of Ranger's training, and hearing more than once that he was on assignment and trusted by the police, that didn't seem like much of a stretch. From what *Hastiin Sani* had told her, the Brotherhood of Warriors were the best of the best and Ranger definitely fit that description.

Dana was intuitively aware of the way he was watching her as she walked inside his home. They were so closely attuned, it was a little bit frightening. Was this love…or was she letting her imagination run wild?

"I need to do something," he said, interrupting her thoughts. "Will you keep an eye on the road we came in on? I don't think we were followed, but I'm not going to underestimate these people."

"No problem."

He took a few steps down the hall, then turned his head. "There's food in the kitchen if you're hungry. You can grab something to eat while you keep watch."

After finding a loaf of wheat bread and some slices of chicken breast and cheese in the kitchen, Dana made two quick sandwiches and left one for Ranger. As she ate her own sandwich, she stood beside the window, looking back in the direction they'd come. The house was at the end of the road, so nobody could come in from another direction except on foot.

Dana heard Ranger moving about in one of the back rooms, but the door was closed and she couldn't make out his conversation. After fifteen minutes he returned.

Seeing him coming down the hall, she called out. "There's a sandwich waiting for you in the kitchen."

"Have you seen anything or anyone?" he asked, coming up from behind her and taking a look for himself.

"Nothing but crows, a cottontail and a ground squirrel. No people, or moving shadows, or cars," she answered. "I was watching on the way here, too. No one followed us."

"These days, with all the electronic gadgets, you don't have to be right on someone's tail to follow them," he warned.

She conceded with a nod. "Have you learned anything we can use?"

"All the men who were in Ernesto Trujillo's original gang have been identified and accounted for. That verifies what we already suspected. Ignacio is recruiting soldiers on his own—mostly small-time locals and off-the-reservation street punks."

"If he's smart, he'll also hire Navajo men who can blend in and pose an even greater threat to us," she said.

Ranger shook his head. "Not likely. We've got… friends. Word has gone out, and the criminal element here on the rez has received a warning they won't ignore. Ignacio won't be able to recruit from inside our borders."

Ranger had left his cell phone on the table next to his keys. When it rang, she handed it to him. From the expression on his face, she could tell that it was very bad news.

Ranger hung up, went to one of the rooms in the back, then returned within a minute carrying a rifle. A pistol was stuck in his belt, and she could see clips of ammunition in his pocket. "We've got to get moving."

"But we just got here."

"The man who stocked the kitchen with food for us was found dead outside a gas station near Shiprock—killed by a sniper while he was gassing up his pickup. The shot apparently came from long range, so it's not likely he gave us up, but it's too risky to stay here now. Others will be watching the road to make sure we're not followed, but you and I need to find another place."

Dana started to ask him for a name, wondering if it had been one on the list, then stopped. That would have also entailed the admission that she knew some of the names. Instead, Dana picked up her bag and went into the kitchen to gather some food and bottled water. "Do you have any idea where we're going, or will we just drive until we get someplace we can hole up for the night?"

Ranger smiled. "That's what I like about you. This isn't your thing—constant changes in plans, and never knowing what's going to happen next— but you adapt quickly."

"I don't have much choice, do I?" she said. They got underway moments later.

They drove east, off the reservation. Finally Ranger broke the silence between them. "Tell me something, Dana. The challenges we've faced, the adventure, does that part appeal to you at all? And will you miss it once it's over?"

"No. In that way we're not at all alike," she said, guessing what was behind his question. "What has kept me going is the hope that we'll find justice for our friend."

"That's important to me, too—both personally and as a Navajo. All things in life are connected and when one thing is out of balance, it affects the whole picture. The only way for any of us to find peace is to restore the *Hohzo,*" he said.

"I understand the concept," she said with a nod. "One of my goals has been to learn more about tra- ditional Navajo ways. Inner peace seems to go hand-in-hand with them."

Ranger nodded. "My mother was a traditionalist. Through her, I learned that words have power, that an eagle feather, a mountain lion skin, or a bear claw can give whoever carries them the strength of that animal. I keep an eagle fetish with me and feed it pollen to keep it strong. Those beliefs make me a Navajo and keep me centered."

She listened, feeling his love for all things Navajo. Defending what he held dear as part of the Brotherhood of Warriors would have come naturally to Ranger.

His cell phone rang again. Seeing his expression remain neutral, she tried to listen to his side of the conversation and figure out what was going on.

A minute later he hung up and met her gaze. "The device inside *Hastiin Dííl'*s hogan was a homemade pipe bomb filled with gunpowder and nails, not another grenade like the one in the medicine hogan. My guess is they didn't have two. The bomb included a lantern battery and an electrical detonator stolen from a construction site about a month ago."

"That means that Trujillo must have been planning his moves for some time—even before he had the names of his future targets," she pointed out.

"Since the death of his brother, probably," he said. "There's a store down the road not too far from here. I'll buy some supplies, then we'll head to higher ground where no one can find us without showing themselves."

How lovely it would have been to share a special place with Ranger where no one could find them for days on end…. The ringing of Ranger's cell phone quickly brought her out of her musings.

Ranger looked at the display and recognized the number. "I'm here, Fire. What's up?" But the voice that answered wasn't his brother's.

"Who am I speaking to?" the voice on the other end demanded.

Ranger pulled the truck over to the side of the highway and focused. "You first, pal."

"This is FBI Agent Harris."

Ranger identified himself immediately. "How did you get the cell phone you're using, Agent Harris?"

"It was the last number dialed on one we found beside the body of another murder victim."

"Victim? *Who?*" Fear pried into him like a knife to the gut. But it couldn't have been his brother. Hunter was too good at what he did. More important, Ranger was sure he would have felt his own twin's death. He was as linked to Hunter as daylight to the sun.

"We haven't ID'd the body yet."

"How did he die?" he asked, his voice thick.

"Sniper took him out with one bullet to the head, apparently. An unidentified witness called in the shooting from a pay phone, and we're trying to track him down," Harris said. "When we arrived at the scene, it took a while to find the exact location the perp used to take the shot. Get this—it was five hundred yards away. We found two sets of footprints and vehicle tracks there."

"Not many people could have made a shot like that," Ranger said, his voice sounding detached.

"I know. That's our best lead. Trujillo's importing talent, either an ex-military marksman, or someone who gets in a lot of practice at the range."

"Two sets of prints suggest a military-style sniper team—spotter and shooter," Ranger said, his voice taut. "Let me know when you've identified the body. The cell phone you've found, I believe, belongs to my brother, Hunter."

"I understand your concern, Blueeyes, and I'll call you personally when we get more information," Harris replied, his voice less official now. Then he ended the call.

Dana saw the beads of sweat that had broken out on Ranger's forehead despite the cool temperature outside. His knuckles were white, a sign of the death grip he had on the steering wheel.

"What's happening?" she asked.

Ranger filled her in with short clipped sentences. "But it couldn't have been my brother. Not many people can guard against a sniper, but my brother would have sensed what was going down. I'm sure of it," he added for his own benefit.

"Other explanations are possible, too. For instance, your brother might have been there, and dropped the phone when the shooting took place. With a sniper in place, it's possible he might not have been able to retrieve it. Or maybe he loaned the phone to the victim and was somewhere else at the time," she said, her tone hopeful. "Don't assume anything. Wait until they confirm the victim's identity."

Ranger tried to push back the darkness that surrounded his every thought, but he couldn't quite do it. If it was true and his brother *was* dead, his own personal hell was just beginning. "The blood that pumps through my brother's veins is the same as mine. He and I are linked. I *would* have felt his death," he repeated firmly.

"Hold to that, then," she said, feeling the edge of desperation that lay behind his words.

He turned up a dirt track that led to the bosque area around the Animas River, not far east from where it joined up with the San Juan. An area free of development, the beauty here was unspoiled, just as nature had intended. He pulled the truck off the irrigation canal road, and down into the dense undergrowth, then shut off the engine.

"We need to hang out for a bit. Here, we'll be out of view and the cell phone will still work. For now, I'd like to stay in contact with Harris." He stared ahead for a second, then slammed his hand hard against the wheel and cursed.

She could feel the darkness building inside him. For the first time since they'd met, Ranger needed her. As someone who'd learned how to cling to hope when there seemed no reason to do so, she could help him now. Ranger needed to find his own strength again and she would be his guide.

"Let's walk down to the river," she suggested.

He nodded. "I know a nice spot against the sandstone hillside, a place where the river has worn a shallow cave into the cliffs. It's not too far. It's deep in the bosque and between two bluffs, so the place is secluded. We should be safe there while we wait."

Taking her hand, Ranger led the way through the maze of cottonwoods, willows and grasses. It never ceased to amaze her how someone as tall and broad-shouldered as Ranger could move so silently through thick vegetation like this.

Later, when they reached the river, he looked in both directions, then led her downstream. Where the cliffs were closest there was a small shelf—a sandbar—that led them into the narrow channel. About fifty feet farther, they came across a small, sandy area along the inside curve of the river. At the base of the cliff was a spot where spring floods had undermined the wall.

Dana sat down beside him on the sandy earth, but

seconds later, he stood and began to pace along the water's edge.

"My brother better be out there, alive and well, or there'll be more blood spilled. I'll make sure of that."

She walked over to where he stood and took his hand. "Concentrate on *life*. Celebrate it. You've always done that by living in the moment. Don't stop now. Life is a gift and not even a moment of it should be wasted."

Dana pulled him to the ground, sat astride him and slid her arms around his neck, molding herself to him. She would give him the comfort only love could bring—a reminder of life in the midst of death. She could think of nothing greater to give the man she'd fallen in love with.

As her lips met his, Ranger returned the kiss fiercely, taking what she offered like a dying man struggling for a breath of air.

She pushed back his shirt and covered his chest with tiny, moist kisses, wanting him. His need pressed intimately against her as her trail of kisses went ever lower down his body. She could feel the fierce pounding of his heart against her palm. She loved touching him and the way his breath sharpened when she caressed him.

"Slow down," he whispered, bringing her face up to meet his lips. Ranger kissed her slowly. In contrast to her hurried movements, he was patient, parting her lips easily, deepening their kiss and letting her take a shaky breath before kissing her again. His voice was gentle as he pushed her hips down against him. "Feel me. I'm ready. But you're not. Not yet."

Steadying her between his arms, Ranger undressed her with unbearable patience, letting his fingertips glide along her breasts, then taking them into his mouth, suckling gently, until she cried out his name.

A whirlwind of emotions ribboned around her. She'd wanted to give comfort but now all she could feel was heat, the searing kind that melted everything in its path. Each nip sent her closer to the brink. Feeling him throbbing beneath her parted legs, she tried to unbuckle his belt, but her fingers were clumsy and her hands shaking.

"If you have any pity in you, you'll help me with this thing," she said, laughing out of sheer frustration.

His chuckle was a throaty growl that sent its ripples all through her. With one quick twist, he undid his belt, then opened his jeans. "Pull them down," he ordered.

Dizzy with needs, she did as he asked because it was exactly what she'd yearned to do. Restraint had covered his body with a sheen of perspiration that accentuated every plane and rise. He was magnificent, his muscled flesh the color of a sunset. She smoothed her hand over him, learning what gave him pleasure.

When the heat became too intense, he gripped her hands and held them to her sides. "My turn," he growled.

He tasted and loved the milky-white softness of her skin, then cupped her intimately, parting the velvety folds, and feeling the moist heat there. When he pressed into her, he could feel everything feminine in her welcoming the intrusion. She strained into him, moaning, and that anguished cry of pure need fueled his own.

Capturing her cries with his mouth, he caressed the center of her womanhood, slowly driving her wild in his arms.

"I can't..."

"Yes, you can. Don't hold back."

His hands were rough and demanding, then tender. Waves of pleasure seared through her until her world came apart in one bright, shining moment. Then, in the safety of his arms, she rested.

Once her breathing evened, he shifted, positioning her beneath him. Passion stronger than anything he'd ever known gripped him.

"Look at me," he demanded and when she did, he gripped her hips and pushed himself into her.

Seeing herself reflected in the black pools of his eyes, she understood the power of harmony and balance.

In a frenzy of need and heat, he drove into her.

Her cries drove him crazy as did the way her fingers dug into his shoulders, almost to the point of pain. In freedom, and in love, their bodies became one, and he poured himself into her.

They lay quietly afterward, her arms and legs still entwined around him. She'd known intimacy before, but never like this. She'd felt as delicate as a flower that had come into bloom in the middle of a storm, and yet powerful, too, knowing she'd given a man like Ranger so much pleasure.

He rolled back, taking her with him, then held her. "You know what's in my heart now," he whispered. "At least in this, there are no secrets."

Dana ached to hear him speak of love, but when he didn't, she held back, too. Ranger was a free spirit, and she'd known that from the beginning. He'd given her all of himself and taken what she'd offered freely, but he would never accept being tied down.

"What I feel for you is real," Ranger said, sensing her feelings. "But I've got nothing else to give you now—no promises or assurances. I haven't got a future—not until I know what happened to my brother, and we finish what needs to be done."

"What we've shared is enough," she whispered. She'd fallen in love and had no regrets. What she'd discovered in his arms would be a part of her forever.

Chapter Sixteen

As they waited for the phone to ring, time passed slowly. Not knowing about his brother's fate was eating Ranger up inside. Waiting was the worst of it, too—trying to hold on to his sanity while being torn between hope and fear.

"Let's go to the police station in Shiprock," she suggested, standing up and walking out toward the river's edge. "They'll get the news there first."

He shook his head. "Too dangerous. There's only one practical route there, and we could easily pick up a tail. We've kept ahead of them so far by going places no one expects us to be." He stood and joined her. "But let's hike back to the truck. This isn't a good place to be once it's dark. We can't see around us beyond the cliffs, and if anyone's tracked us, the rushing water will cover the sound of their approach."

"Where else can we go?"

"I know of another place. We'll be safe there, and

it'll give me a chance to figure out who I can use as our contact now."

"Your brother was the one you were calling, and who'd been contacting you?"

"Most of the time."

"Okay, so where's this new place?"

"It's not a place as much as a location up in the mountains. That's where I was originally headed when Harris called. We'll be able to spot any vehicle from miles away. And if they come on foot, it'll take them hours to reach us."

"Will you get phone service there?" she asked.

"It won't be as reliable as it is here but, yeah, I think so."

"Considering you're waiting for news, are you sure that's worth it?"

"It's the only place I'm sure we can be safe tonight," he answered.

They drove south from Farmington for almost an hour and a half, reaching the reservation community of Crownpoint. Then they turned south down graveled roads, heading southwest into the mountains around the Continental Divide. Twice, he was sure they'd picked up a tail, but after a circuitous route along dirt roads, he couldn't see any signs of a vehicle tailing them.

"Keep an eye out for a tail," he said.

"I have been, but no one's stuck with us."

At long last, they came upon a big rockslide that covered many acres along the flank of a mountain. At first Dana thought it might have been an old mine site. But a closer look revealed no roads, buildings or machinery, and the stones all seemed to have originated from the cliffs above. Soon they topped a ridge that jutted out of the mountainside like a shoulder, and the road finally leveled off.

The ridge joined with the rocky cliff. Small caves and crevices dotted the mountain side opposite the slope, and only a few trees and shrubs were tenacious enough to hug the thin soil at this elevation.

Ranger pulled up as close to the cliff as possible, then turned the pickup sideways to the mountain, coming to rest between a grove of pines and the rock wall. They'd be hidden from anyone coming up the mountain, at least until they got very close.

"We'll camp here for the night. It's safer than anywhere else I can think of," he said, "and any approaching vehicles will make quite a bit of noise coming across that rubble below."

Dana got out of the truck and looked around, taking a deep breath. The view below them in the reddish, late-afternoon sun was beautiful, with the desert valley spread out for many miles to the north, and the Chuska Mountains to the west. It felt as if they were sitting on top of the world.

"My cell phone is operable up here, thanks to all

the mining operations just to the south," he said, after checking to verify.

As Dana drew closer to the edge of the cliff, she got a glimpse of a rare sight. "There's an eagle's nest up here," she whispered quickly. "Maybe we should move back down the mountain a little. I'd hate to disturb it."

As Ranger looked down at the eagle perched on her nest, his voice rose in a soft chant that seemed to warm the cold breeze. It was a haunting song that reverberated with power and mystery.

The eagle didn't move, and Ranger smiled. "Her children have already left the nest and are on their own. The eagle knows it has nothing to fear from us. She'll be our eyes, and if anyone tries to come after us, she'll let us know."

As Dana looked at the eagle the huge raptor stirred in her nest, but didn't fly away. Moving back slowly, Dana gazed at Ranger. "It's almost like you have a connection with her. I can't believe she's so calm."

He reached into the *jish* he carried on his belt and brought out an eagle fetish carved of stone. "The eagle and I are linked spiritually."

It fit him—that boundless love of freedom, the ability to survive despite the odds. "You're two of a kind," she said at last.

Dana zipped up her jacket, and rubbed her arms

for warmth. The altitude, the breeze and the fact that it was November promised a cold night.

"Come here," he whispered, opening his jacket, then pulling her against his own body. "I'll keep you warm."

As he held her, they watched the eagle fly off, spin and turn gracefully in the air, swoop down, then return to her old nest, her dinner clutched in powerful talons.

"Graceful, isn't she? She can gauge the currents and soar above them effortlessly," he said.

It was then that she truly began to understand Ranger. He saw his ability to challenge the winds of change as the road to harmony and happiness. In contrast, she'd always seen home and her familiar routines as the path to security and well-being. But all those had ever given her was the *illusion* of safety.

Before she could think about this further, she heard Ranger's cell phone ring and saw him answer, clutching the small phone hard in his hand. A heartbeat later, he grinned widely and Dana knew Ranger's brother was alive.

EXCITEMENT AND RELIEF swept through Ranger as he heard his brother's voice.

"I'm in one piece" came the announcement from Hunter.

"What's happened?" Ranger asked. "All I knew

was that your cell had been found next to an un-identified victim."

"The sniper took out one of our people. I was there, managed to follow and track them, and got the spotter—the other half of the sniper team. But I lost the cell phone and, until now, I didn't have a way to contact you."

"The spotter…is he dead?"

"He died from his wounds, but not before he talked. He said you're not the target, the woman is, which means they haven't confirmed who you are. But they've been tracking you via the GPS system in your truck. They have an informant in the company that manufactured it, courtesy of Trujillo's money. They know *exactly* where you are now."

"We're in a secure location," Ranger insisted.

"I know how you think, and I've got a good idea of where you are. But, Wind, this sniper is *good.* He's got military training—the way he teamed up with a spotter proves that. He's also a master at camouflage. I only saw him after he'd taken the shot. If he comes after you, you may never see him coming."

"Did you?"

There was a pause. "No, but I sensed him, which is why I'm the one who survived his attack."

"I'll be ready."

After he hung up, Ranger pulled Dana down into a shady spot, lowering their profile by half, and filled her in on the conversation. "The best way to survive a sniper's attack is to be more patient than he is. We'll need a good hiding place where we can lay low. He can only shoot at what he sees. A sniper keys on your movements. If we can outlast him, it'll be his own movements that'll reveal his location."

"You have a rifle with a scope. How accurate are you with that thing?"

"I can hit a soup can at three hundred yards nine out of ten times. I'm accurate on larger targets beyond that range, too, depending on the wind, the lighting and other variables. But keep in mind that this man will have a lot more experience than I do factoring in the conditions. He's supposed to be a master when it comes to camouflage, too. He won't be easy to spot, and forget about hearing him. He'll move slowly and carefully once he locates the pickup."

Ranger brought out his binoculars and surveyed the area below.

"Do you see him?" she asked after several minutes had gone by.

"No, but I can feel him down there. He'll work his way up slowly through the rockslide, from shadow to shadow. It's what I would do." He took a deep breath then chanted softly. "In the trail of beauty…" he began and as his voice rose above a whisper, the eagle stirred and took flight.

She soared free, turning in a tight circle, then

swooped down over an outcropping where boulders the size of truck tires had tumbled down the mountain. She dove almost to the surface, then turned sharply, catching an updraft and spiraling up into the sky. She then glided back to her cliffside nest with little effort.

"Ahéhee'," he said, thanking her, but his words were nothing more than a stirring in the wind.

"Did you…did she…no, that's impossible… isn't it?"

Ranger never answered. He trained his binoculars on the area the eagle had pinpointed for him. He watched for perhaps five minutes, holding perfectly still. "Got you now," he muttered at last.

"You saw him?"

"He's hidden among the rocks at the lower end of that outcropping. All I caught was a flicker of movement as he crawled from one shadow to the next. But that was enough. My guess is that he already knows where we are, too, or at least where we went, and he's angling for a clear line of sight."

"So what do we do? We can't stay up here forever," she said, "and if we drive back down, we'll go right past him."

"We'll need to draw him out. I won't be able to get a shot where he is right now."

"I can't shoot, but I can get his attention," she said, forcing her voice to remain firm and clasping her hands together so he couldn't see them shaking. "When he gets close enough to take a shot at me, just get him first."

"No."

"Is there another way?"

He paused. "Not that I can think of right off the bat."

"Then we have no choice," she said.

"It's too risky. Forget it."

"I'm not a risk taker. You already know that. But I trust you. We can set him up. To take a shot at me he'll have to expose himself. You won't miss. Now tell me how to make that happen," she said.

He said nothing for several long moments. "There's one way to do this without placing you in any more danger than you're already in. We'll go up onto the ridge, letting him see us only long enough for the movement to register in his vision— a second, nothing more. We'll have to make it look casual, like we don't have a clue he's out there and we're just talking. Once we're behind cover and can't be seen anymore, I want you to keep talking, like we're still together. And light a small fire, too—like we're keeping warm, so he can register on the smoke and the sound."

Ranger stood, slung the rifle over his shoulder and took her hand. "Let's move now. Don't look back, but don't stop, either."

She followed him closely, fighting the urge to look back where the sniper had been just a few minutes ago. "Where will you be?"

"I'm going to circle around, figure out where he'll have to position himself to shoot at you and wait to ambush him. You need to sit down low and place the rifle to your left with the barrel up."

"If he sees the rifle, he'll think you're with me...?"

"Exactly. As a sniper, he'll never believe I've given up my long-range weapon, particularly in terrain like this where it would be most effective."

"You'll have your pistol, right?"

Ranger nodded, then slipped a small lighter into her pocket, and handed her the rifle. "Make that small fire using sticks and branches you can reach without getting up again. If it burns out, okay, it's just for show, anyway. Under no circumstances do you stand up or move from your position until I come to get you."

"I might be able to use this rifle, but how will I know if you need help?" she asked.

"I appreciate the offer, but stick with the plan." He pointed to a low spot in the rocks that over-looked the landslide below. A stunted evergreen stood at the far side. "That's a good spot for you." He stopped, then brought out the cell phone and handed it to her. "Order us a pizza."

She smiled. "Just come back, okay?"

"Always. Gotta go, so keep talking."

Ranger moved off quickly and disappeared behind some trees that had managed to grab hold in the rocky ridge.

Trying to keep her voice from cracking as she talked, Dana went to the spot among the rocks, the rifle her only companion.

ALTHOUGH HE'D HATED leaving Dana with danger closing in, he'd had no other choice. He moved silently, listening to messages from Wind. Since the breeze was blowing toward him, he would be able to hear even the slightest shift in the rocks and coarse gravel, but his opponent wouldn't.

Ranger moved downhill and to the right, taking a position in the recess below a rock overhang where he'd be hidden from anyone approaching from downhill. Taking out his .45 pistol, Ranger released the safety, crouched low, then waited, absolutely still. In the distance, he could hear Dana's voice, though her words were indistinguishable.

Time passed slowly. Ranger couldn't risk a look down at his watch, but he noted the change in shadow lengths as the sun dropped lower toward the western horizon. It would be dark before long, and though the sniper was obviously being very careful, the man would have to make his move before then.

Studying the area, he spotted a shadow up ahead between him and where Dana was now sitting. Then he saw the brim of his enemy's boonie cap. As quietly as he could, Ranger raised his pistol and squeezed the trigger. The sound was deafening, not just the blast of the pistol, but the clang as the big .45 slug struck the receiver of the sniper's rifle.

Ranger was out of the hole within two seconds, his pistol pointed right into the eyes of the sniper. He heard the clank of his opponent's rifle as it hit the ground, but Ranger's gaze stayed on his sights and the man's sweating face just beyond.

"On your knees, hands locked behind your head," Ranger ordered. Then, moving to the side, he took the sniper's knife out of its sheath. Ranger circled the man, searching for any other weapons that might be visible, then had the man empty his pockets and remove his bootlaces so he couldn't run anywhere easily.

"Dana, it's okay now. Come help me secure the prisoner," he called out.

She was there within two minutes, breathing hard, a smile of relief on her face. As she pointed the rifle at the sniper, Ranger used the handcuffs the man had carried in his pockets, no doubt to secure Dana, to position his prisoner's hands behind his back. He took the handcuff key off the key ring and put it in his own pocket.

Once the prisoner was secured, Ranger got his cell phone back from Dana and contacted his brother, who'd already sent backup from Thoreau, a small community to the south.

"A tribal officer and the state police are coming up the mountain and will soon be joining you and take custody of the prisoner," his brother said. "Once you've handed him over, go back to Shiprock via Gallup. You'll need to meet with Agent Harris. Xander Glint, the man involved in the original kidnap plot, is now out of ICU and able to talk."

"Has he said anything?"

"Not from what I've heard. But once you're on the scene you'll know more."

Dana handed Ranger his rifle, then walked over and stood in front of the sniper. She met his expressionless gaze and held it. "You weren't involved in the kidnapping, but you're still a killer," she said, then slapped him hard. "That's for hiring out to the man who murdered a dear friend of mine."

The man spat out a curse and tried to stand, but Ranger brought his rifle up and aimed it at the man's forehead. "Don't even think it."

The man froze, then sagged back down to his knees, his head lowered.

"You're getting off easy," Dana said. As she looked over at Ranger, all she saw on his face was approval…and admiration.

Chapter Seventeen

Two hours had passed since they'd turned over their prisoner to the officers. They were driving north on the main highway when Ranger's cell phone rang. Even without looking he knew it would be his brother.

Ranger listened to what Hunter had to say, then answered. "That's good to hear," he said. He hung up, then glanced over at Dana and brought her up to date.

"It seems our sniper, who'll only give his first name—Willie—is more than eager to spill his guts. But he wants to deal."

"Let's go see if we can listen in on the interrogation. Maybe I can help somehow. We should be safe there, too. Trujillo won't come for me at the station."

As she said it, Dana realized how much she'd changed. Faced with nonstop danger and unpredictability, she'd found new strength. Dana glanced over at Ranger, who looked as tired as she felt, and began to see their relationship in a new light.

Although what was happening between them held no guarantees of a happily ever after, life was offering her a precious gift—but it wasn't forcing it on her. She could accept it, or walk away as soon as she could.

"We've become a good team," Ranger said, his eyes on the road, but his hand reaching over to cover her own.

She smiled. "I know you're more comfortable acting off-the-cuff, but I've got to give you credit. You can certainly come up with a plan when it's needed."

"Back there, my one priority was keeping you safe. That took planning. Had it been just me, I might have handled it differently. But you were involved and that changed everything."

A rainbow of warm, gentle feelings filled her. "I couldn't have asked for a better guardian."

"I know. I'm a man of many talents," he said with a wicked grin, his voice low and seductive.

"Yes, but where would you be without the inspiration I provide?" she answered, trying to keep a straight face.

He laughed, a booming, deep sound that was infectious.

The drive back was uneventful and long. When they finally pulled into the Shiprock police station Dana sat up and gestured ahead.

"There's the sniper," she said.

The prisoner, his feet in shackles and his hands cuffed in front now, was being escorted into the building by a state police officer and a tribal cop.

Ranger and Dana went in a moment later and found Agent Harris waiting for them in the lobby. "The prisoner is being taken to an interrogation room, and I'm going to question him myself," he said. "The deal he wants isn't going to happen, but if he wants to avoid a potential life sentence, his only choice is to cooperate. I'll bring that up, and hope he sees the light."

"I hear Xander Glint is conscious now, too," Ranger said.

Harris nodded. "Once we're through here, we'll head to the hospital."

Twenty minutes later, Dana and Ranger stood outside the one-way glass as Harris questioned the seated suspect, who was without handcuffs now but still wearing leg irons.

Harris rose from his own chair, walked around the room once, then stopped abruptly and leaned over the prisoner. "Your prints are being processed, and your photo is being taken to every gun dealer in the area. You'll be recognized, and if you have a rap sheet, we'll know that, too. So why don't you stop wasting my time? What's your real name—all of it."

"William George Franklin," he answered. "Willie."

"Okay, Willie. Who hired you?"

"Hired? Nobody hired me," he countered. "I was out hunting ground squirrels when some Indian with a forty-five ambushed me. He shot at me, held a pistol to my head, then tied me up. Then he called in some cop friends, and they hauled me here on some phony assault charge. Is anyone taking care of my Jeep? I left it parked down the mountain a few miles. If it gets stolen, I'm going to sue that Indian and his entire tribe."

"We've got an eyewitness that saw you leaving a murder scene with a rifle. That witness's testimony will carry some serious weight. He was the one who neutralized your spotter," he said, careful not to use Hunter Blueeyes's name. "I also have two more people here at the station who'll happily testify against you—the pair that you were stalking up in the mountains before they brought you down. The bullets that killed two Navajo men have been recovered, too, and once we match them to your rifle, you're looking at life in prison. So what'll it be? Turn state's evidence now, or rot in prison for the rest of your life?"

"I want full immunity before I say anything else."

"I want to win the lottery. It looks like we're both out of luck," Harris spat out.

"Then forget about it. I'm not saying another word until I talk to a lawyer. I know my rights."

Dana watched him, anger seething inside her. "I've about had it with this jerk," she whispered furiously.

Ranger chuckled softly. "Easy. Let Harris work a little longer. He's got a reputation for getting things done. He's just got his own style, that's all."

Dana focused on the two men inside the room. Harris walked back to his chair, sat down, then leaned back casually.

"You'll be serving time—hard time, and most likely in a federal prison. I can't do anything about that, but twenty years, even twenty-five, is better than life. Ten minutes of truth can save you decades in a cell with a mean, ugly, sweaty roommate named Chuck. Give me a reason to tell the DA that you cooperated. That's my final offer."

"Yeah, that and three-fifty will get me a cup of coffee," Willie spat out. "Do your best. You've got nothing on me but lies."

"You're going down, Franklin, and you know it as well as I do."

Willie held Harris's gaze, then finally his eyes narrowed. "If I decide to cooperate, will I get protection?"

"You'll be guarded around the clock until we put the ones you're working for behind bars."

Willie leaned forward, resting his elbows on the

desk between them. "I know you want a name, but I never asked and he never offered one."

Harris reached into his jacket pocket and brought out three photos, laying them on the table in front of Willie. "Is the man who hired you among these?"

Willie glanced down and picked out the photo on the end. "That's him, but he's older now, and has a mustache. After he handed over half the money, he said I'd have someone watching me while I worked. If I failed to kill the bodyguard and take the woman—by tonight—I'd be as good as dead."

Dana looked over at Ranger. "That's why he had the handcuffs," she whispered. "You were supposed to be killed. I was going to be kidnapped again."

Ranger nodded, remembering his brother's report.

They both looked back through the glass as Harris continued.

"He can't get at you here. You'll be in a tribal jail cell by yourself," Harris said, holding up Ignacio Trujillo's photo so they could see it on the other side of the glass.

"No, man, you don't get it. The dude's bad, and he's rich. He's got bodyguards who'll slit your throat for a six-pack of warm beer. With his money he'll find someone willing to stick a screwdriver in my back."

"Not here, and especially not once we lock him and his people up. That's where you come in. We're going to need everything you have on him—how he contacts you, what he's driving, all those details."

"Fine, but not before my lawyer gets here," Willie said. "He'll make sure I'm not screwed out of anything I should have."

"Okay. I'll let you know when he arrives. Until then you're going to a holding cell. You'll be alone, so no one can get you there." Harris opened the door and waved to an officer coming down the hall. "Officer Benally, would you escort the prisoner to lockup while I speak with your captain?"

"Sure." Officer Benally waved Franklin out from behind the desk. "Turn around, please," Benally said, taking the handcuffs off his belt.

Willie held out one hand, but when Benally reached for the other wrist, the prisoner whirled around and tried to grab Benally's pistol.

Ranger moved in to help, but Harris got there first. He clipped Willie on the side of his head with the heel of his palm.

Franklin, his balance precarious with his ankles shackled, fell hard, dropping the pistol when his head bounced off the seat of Harris's wooden chair. There was a sickening crunch as he hit the floor, face first.

Willie's body started to twitch, his head at an unnatural angle.

Dana stared in horror through the glass, her heart

hammering against her ribs. Benally flew out into the hall, yelling for help. Dana saw blood flowing onto the floor. She watched mesmerized, as Willie's body twitched hard one more time, then lay motionless.

Dana turned away, feeling weak and a little sick to her stomach. No matter where she went, death was waiting. She was trapped in a circle of violence with no way out.

Ranger pulled her into his arms. "Franklin made his choice," he said softly. "At least no one else was hurt."

Seeing Harris motioning to them, Dana stepped out of Ranger's arms and walked down the hall toward the agent. As she did, she took deep breaths, trying to pull herself together. She wouldn't let herself fall apart now.

"I don't know why Willie reacted like that. It cost him his life," Harris said as they joined him. "I *told* him he'd be in one of our holding cells, away from even other inmates, but he still tried to escape."

"Where does that leave you now?" Ranger asked.

"We've got one more potential informant— Xander Glint. I've got guards all around him but, so far, Glint's not talking."

"I've got an idea," Dana said. "Let me go identify him for you, face-to-face. Once he knows his conviction is all but guaranteed, that may jolt him into cooperating."

"It's worth a shot," Harris said. "I'll let the guards know you're coming, and join you there."

As they walked back outside, Dana couldn't help wondering if they'd make it to the finish line in one piece. Trujillo was a relentless enemy. As long as he remained free she'd never be able to go back to her life. She missed her work, her students, the sanity of routines. Yet, deep down, she also knew that her eventual return would be bittersweet. Nothing would ever be the same for her again.

She glanced at Ranger, lost in her own thoughts. Her one wish was that Ranger would choose to remain a part of her life even after the danger had passed. But wishes alone would never tame the wind.

Chapter Eighteen

Ranger parked toward the north end of the regional medical center in the city of Farmington. This was where Glint, a non-Navajo, had been transferred after being stabilized.

Focused on security, Ranger studied the area around them before turning off the engine. It was close to midnight and quiet at this late hour. There had been very little traffic, even on major streets. The powerful lights that illuminated the parking lot made for few shadows, and because it was long after visiting hours, most of the vehicles probably belonged to the staff.

Though he could see nothing out of the ordinary, something didn't feel right. The skin at the back of his neck prickled, and he studied all the vehicles he could see, especially unmarked vans.

A strong breeze rose in the air, and a small whirlwind came to life just outside the truck, stirring up dust and leaves. As Dana started to open the door, he pulled her back. "That's an ill wind and it brings bad luck. Wait until it passes."

Dana nodded and sat back. The fact that she'd accepted what he'd said without question pleased him. She wasn't Navajo, but she respected Navajo ways. A man could spend a lifetime looking for a woman like Dana—one who could understand what couldn't be explained.

They left the truck moments later. His muscles tense, he stepped in front of her, and led the way quickly toward the closest entrance.

"What's wrong?" she asked.

"Stay on your guard. Something's not right."

Yards from the side door, Ranger heard running footsteps, and two men emerged from behind a row of parked cars to his left, cutting off their retreat. A third man suddenly stepped around the last car on the right, placing himself between them and the hospital doors.

Dana stopped abruptly, seeing the men closing in from all sides.

"Run for the door," Ranger said, then rushed the man in their way, though his opponent was built like a human roadblock.

Unwilling to leave Ranger alone to fight three men, Dana turned and kicked one of the men coming up from behind. As she turned toward the other guy who was behind Ranger, she realized he was pulling out a handgun.

Ranger, busy fighting the big guy, had his back turned. Dana yelled out, warning Ranger as she dove for the pistol and knocked it out of the man's hand. There was a loud pop as the weapon flew across the lane, sliding beneath a red car.

The man cursed, clutching his hand, and staggered back, looking for his weapon. Ranger hurled his opponent over his shoulder, slamming him into the pavement. Dana kicked the shins of the smaller man, the one she'd kicked first.

Out of the corner of her eye, she saw the third man, having given up on the pistol, trying to decide who to attack, her or Ranger. Then seeing the big man down, flat on his back, he suddenly bolted, along with his partner. Within seconds they were halfway across the parking lot, racing toward a shiny new pickup.

"Maybe they saw we were getting some help," Dana said, and pointed. Agent Harris was running toward them, two security guards behind him.

As two of their assailants sped away, Ranger cursed, then quickly focused back on the third man, who was still on the pavement, moaning.

The downed man groaned in defeat as Harris and the two security guards teamed up to handcuff him, then hauled him to his feet.

"Do you recognize this guy?" Harris asked

Dana, who shook her head after taking a closer look at the man's blood-smeared face.

Harris looked at Ranger, who also shook his head. Immediately the agent read the man his rights and flashed his Bureau ID. "Do yourself a favor and don't piss me off," he growled after he'd finished. "What's your name and who sent you?"

"Name's Truman Ockerman," he said, mumbling. "I was just here to rough up the Indian because he owes the wrong people a chunk of change," he said, looking at Ranger.

"Wrong. Try again," Ranger shot back.

"Who hired you?" Harris repeated.

"The two wimps who just ran off," Truman grumbled. "I'm a pro wrestler, but I got hurt and that put me out of work for a while. Hey, I gotta eat just like everyone else."

"I'm going to ask you this one last time. I want names. *Who hired you?*" Harris said through clenched teeth.

"I don't *know.* I met them at the Terminal Café barely an hour ago. They told me what they wanted, then paid me a hundred down in cash. It wasn't supposed to be a big deal. We'd wait here until you two came to visit a sick friend, slap you around a bit, scare the woman, then toss you both into a trash bin."

"What about the gunshot? That suggests the plan included more than a beating," Harris snapped.

"They changed the plan at the last minute. I was supposed to clock this dude while they took the woman back to their pickup for who knows what. I'm no pervert, so I figured I'd just deck the guy, then split."

"You're involved in an attempted murder," Ranger growled. "One of your buddies was about to shoot me when my partner stepped up and knocked away his pistol." He glanced at Harris then added, "It slid beneath that red Chevy. There's the brass from the round he got off," Ranger added, pointing at the ejected shell casing on the pavement.

Dana looked at Ranger, her stomach in knots as she remembered. He'd made it sound so matter-of-fact but the truth was she'd been terrified she'd be seconds too late.

"Guns, shooting people. None of that was *my* idea. It's the truth, I'm telling you," Ockerman said as one of the security men led him away.

Harris bent down and aimed a penlight beneath the red car. "Looks like a thirty-two." The agent pulled a latex glove from his jacket pocket, then picked up the shell casing and examined it closely. "You both still in one piece?"

Ranger looked at Dana, who nodded, then focused back on Harris, who was placing the spent cartridge into a small envelope.

"Anything from Glint so far?" Ranger asked.

"Nothing," Harris said. "Let me collect the weapon, then we'll go inside."

Ranger stood beside Dana and gave her hand a squeeze while the agent retrieved the pistol and stowed it away.

"Your people haven't made much headway, Agent Harris. So how about letting me take the lead once we're in Glint's room?" Dana asked, letting go of Ranger's hand once they reached the hospital door.

Ranger rammed his hands in his pockets and shrugged when Harris glanced over at him. "If I were you, I'd let her have a shot. The lady's got good instincts. She saved my butt tonight."

"I've learned a lot these past few days, Agent Harris," Dana said as they passed a nurses' station. "You've got nothing to lose."

"Go for it." Harris nodded at the two guards standing by the closed door of Room 122, then led the way inside.

Xander Glint was a barrel-chested man with hairy arms, one of them hooked up to an IV, the other handcuffed to a bed rail. Despite the fact that he was propped up in bed, he was still defiant, and glared at them as they came through the doorway. When he saw Dana, he smiled, showing a missing tooth and a split lip just starting to heal.

"I just love this hospital—providing a woman of the evening to comfort me. Give us a half hour alone, okay, guys?" he said, leering at Dana. "And somebody close the door as you go."

Ranger's gaze slashed through him like razor blades. "You working to be unconscious again, loudmouth?"

Dana stepped in front of Ranger and moved closer to the bed, taking a good, long look at Glint's face.

"I know you," she said quietly. "He's definitely one of the kidnappers," she added, looking over at Harris, who nodded.

Glint shook his head. "One of who? I've never seen you before, lady."

"Yes, you have—back at the cabin. You remember *me,* I can see it in your eyes." She glanced at Harris again. "No doubt at all in my mind, Agent Harris. This is one of the men who kidnapped the medicine man and me, and is responsible for his murder. I'll gladly testify to that at his trial."

"This woman is nuts—or blind," Glint said, sitting upright now.

Harris smiled. "Looks to me like you're finally going down, Glint. It won't take a jury fifteen minutes to convict you. The medicine man's murder may even get you the chair instead of life without parole. If I were you, I'd start talking. It's the only chance you've got."

"People who spill their guts to the cops end up dead," he spat out. "I'll take my chances in court."

"Flowers…" Dana commented, looking down at the daisies on the nightstand. "I wonder if the woman who sent them knows you won't be getting out before she's old and gray? She won't even remember what you looked like, if you ever make parole, that is."

"Forget the sob story, I have no idea how those flowers got here. They probably got the wrong room. Now get out, all of you," Glint said. "I want a lawyer."

Dana studied the flowers for a moment, then took out the small notebook from her purse. As the men's attention became focused on her, Dana turned the pad around and showed Glint what she'd written.

Don't talk. There's some kind of electronic bug in your flowers, she wrote.

Glint raised off the bed and peered over as she pointed it out to him. He turned and gave Harris an obscene gesture.

"Not mine," Harris said, taking a closer look.

Your boss doesn't trust you. You're a dead man, Dana wrote.

Glint looked around the room like a trapped man, then finally focused on Agent Harris. Wild-eyed, he signaled for some paper. "I'm not talking," he said, directing his words at the flowers.

Won't matter. You're a liability, Dana wrote.

Ranger, who'd looked in the basket, moved to pick it up, but Harris held up his hand, warning him away.

Agent Harris nodded to Dana, and she handed Glint her notepad and pen.

Do you know Ignacio Trujillo? Harris wrote.

Just Ernesto, and he's dead, came Glint's reply.

Harris brought out three photos, one being of Ignacio Trujillo, but Glint shook his head at each photo.

Who were your contacts? Harris wrote.

Marc Finch and a guy named Del. Don't know his last name, the injured prisoner wrote back.

Harris took the pad. Describe them.

Take the flowers out of here first, Glint wrote back, looking nervously at the flowers.

I'll put them in another room, Dana wrote. Your boss won't catch on right away.

Once Ranger had made a show of taking the bouquet out of the room, Glint began to give them detailed descriptions.

AFTERWARD, they met outside in the hall. After walking some distance away from Glint's door, Harris looked at Dana through narrowed eyes.

"What the heck was that all about?" he asked. "I looked right into the middle of that flower arrangement, but didn't see a thing. Where was the bug?"

"Actually, I think it was somebody's button. I just decided to play a bluff," she said. "You learn to do that in a classroom when you're tracking down which student hid the handle to the pencil sharpener."

"Inspired tactic, Ms. Seles," Harris said. "Now stay out of my case. Law enforcement officers will take it from here. Good night." Harris strode back to Glint's room.

WITH HARRIS GONE, Ranger grabbed Dana's hand, and led her back outside in a hurry. "I need to make a phone call. Let's see if I can get some information on Marc Finch and Del," he said, punching out a number.

Ranger reported in to his brother quickly. "Do we have any information on these guys? More specifically, did Ernesto Trujillo ever use them?" There was a long pause at the other end.

"Wind, you still there?" came Hunter's voice two minutes later.

"Yeah."

"The two guys weren't connected to Ernesto, according to our former inside man. We know Ignacio must be hiring new talent. Finch is a low-rent hood, according to my best source, but he doesn't have an arrest record beyond high school. Nothing on anyone named Del. If I had a last name…"

"Can you track down a photo of Marc Finch for me?"

"Might take awhile. We'll put feelers out, but our manpower is limited. Only those currently known to *Hastiin Dííl* are in play."

Feeling frustrated, Ranger hung up and hurried back to the truck with her. "Let's put some distance between us and this hospital. I don't want a second team sneaking up on us."

"Every time we get close to Ignacio, he slithers out of our grasp. All we get is hired muscle."

"Ignacio is smart, and deadly. But we'll get him," Ranger said.

"How? By going after this Finch guy?"

"We don't have squat on anyone named Del, so that makes Marc Finch our best lead," he answered. "I want to check all the cheap motels in this area. Let's see if they've got a guest using the name Finch, or something close to that."

"These businesses aren't just going to hand us their guest lists—we're not the police, and we don't have a warrant."

"There's a faster way. I've got a laptop beneath your seat that's got all kinds of special software and hardware for satellite access. I can hack into the servers that control most reservation and ticketing venues. It's a read-only connection, but that's all we need. It'll just take me a few minutes to get set up." He pulled off the road then and taking the laptop, moved his seat back and began to work.

"Will you be able to retrieve the information before they catch on to you?" she asked.

"Probably, but there's a certain amount of risk involved. It isn't exactly legal," he added, giving her a quirky grin.

"Neither is kidnapping and murder. Go for it," she said.

He smiled. No wonder he was crazy about her. "You're terrific."

"I'm just tired of playing by the rules. For the first time in my life I'm willing to get a little reckless. Think you're a bad influence?"

"I hope so," he said with a grin, then grew serious. "But, for the record, I'm *never* reckless. I'm willing to take calculated risks. There's a difference."

She nodded thoughtfully, then said, "The biggest difference between us is that I'm willing to do what has to be done, but you love the danger."

"Danger is all around us. Somebody has to meet it head-on so others can walk in beauty."

She was beginning to understand him. Like Icarus, he soared high, letting the winds carry him dangerously close to the sun because everything in him demanded he try, even when the odds were against him. It was courage in its rawest and most dazzling form. She was more sure than ever that he was a member of the Brotherhood of Warriors.

Chapter Nineteen

Dana watched him work, questions racing through her head. At long last she spoke. "That's some special software. How did you get it?"

"Friends," he answered, his gaze never leaving the screen.

"These friends…are they part of the Brotherhood of Warriors?" she asked, then, to her horror, realized she'd spoken the question out loud. But it was too late to take it back now.

"What do you know about the brotherhood?" he asked, again not taking his eyes off the screen.

"Not much more than their name, and the fact that they stay in the shadows."

"Then asking about it would be pointless, wouldn't it?" he countered with a trace of a smile.

"Yeah." There it was. That constant reminder that no matter how close they became, there would always be barriers between them.

"What's bothering you—your secrets or mine?

Nobody can know another person completely. In your heart, you already know all you need to."

"Maybe so." Loving a man like Ranger meant accepting that a part of him would always remain hidden...out of her reach. Yet the closeness her heart yearned for, the kind that would form a bond that could never be broken, would demand more from both of them.

"I got a hit," he said suddenly. "One of the lodges near Stoner, Colorado, northeast of Dolores, recently rented a room to a guest named I. M. Finch."

"I've been to that lodge a few times. It's only an hour's drive from here. So what now?"

"I know the lady who works the night desk... well, her sister. Let me call and see if the description is a match."

Ranger dialed and after exchanging some pleasantries got the information. "It's a match to the description we got from Xander Glint," he told Dana. "Definitely worth the drive."

"When do you plan to tell Agent Harris?" she asked, then reading his expression added, "You *are* planning on telling him, right?"

He shook his head. "I don't want to take a chance on losing this guy. Finch is the closest lead we've had to Trujillo so far, and the only reason we have it is because I cut corners. The FBI plays by the rules and that ties their hands. The first question Harris will ask me is how I got this information. If that happens, things will get complicated and it could end up costing us a very important lead. Will you trust me and let me handle this my way?"

In her heart, she longed to say yes, to agree totally and, for once, let go of all sense of responsibility. But she'd always followed her highest sense of justice, and this was no time to turn away from that. "How about a compromise, one that'll keep us from obstructing the law?" she said at last. "You can wait awhile on Agent Harris, but sometime before we get there, one of us will make the call."

"Deal."

BY THE TIME THEY reached the resort it was nearly 3:00 a.m., and dark everywhere except for the river, which reflected the moonlight like a silver ribbon. They'd called Harris on the way, and Ranger knew that it was likely local law enforcement had beaten them there.

As Ranger turned onto the lane leading to the lodge, they heard a gunshot. Dana sat bolt upright in her seat.

Ranger took his pistol out of his belt and rested it on the cushion beside him as he raced up the graveled road. At the end of the pathway, he could see the lodge's well-lit parking lot. A Montezuma

County sheriff's department cruiser was parked in front of a guest room.

Ranger pulled in slowly, alert for trouble. "The deputy's door is open, but where is he?"

As they got closer Ranger spotted the downed officer on the gravel, his body hidden by the shade of the building. An instant later, they heard the roar of a car engine and the rattle of gravel. Dust flew up as a small sedan roared past them, heading down the long drive toward the highway.

Cursing, Ranger pulled up beside the downed officer's car. "We can't leave him. He's injured," he said, jumping out.

Seeing a light come on outside the lodge entrance, and a man sticking his head out the door, Ranger yelled out, "Call 911. An officer's injured."

"Okay," came the response, and the man disappeared back inside.

Ranger bent down beside the officer, looking for signs of life and evidence of any wounds. There was a hole in the center of the deputy's uniform shirt, but no blood. More lights came on as guests turned on porch lights and peered out their doors.

Then the officer stirred and sat up. "Man, that hurts!" he said, rubbing his chest.

Dana, who was looking over Ranger's shoulder, gave the officer a big smile.

"Wearing a vest?" Ranger asked quickly.

"Yeah. Wife insists. Good thing. Did you get a look at the shooter?"

"No, but I'm going after him right now." Ranger grabbed Dana's hand, and ran back to his pickup.

Moments later, they were back on the highway. The dust cloud and skid marks showed the shooter had gone north at the junction, which would take him farther into the mountains.

Ranger made the turn smoothly, but the force yanked Dana sideways in her shoulder belt and she grabbed onto the seat.

"Those are his taillights," Ranger said, accelerating even more. "Just hang on, we'll catch him."

Dana kept her eyes forward, concentrating on keeping the red taillights of Finch's car in view. They were gaining ground.

"We're chasing Marc Finch, right? Not somebody else who had a beef with the deputy?" she asked, her voice sounding a little high-pitched, even to herself. Although Ranger was an excellent driver, they were traveling at close to one hundred miles per hour.

"I don't believe in coincidences," Ranger replied, his eyes never leaving the road.

Ahead, she saw a triangular orange sign—a warning of a construction zone. The speeding car in front of them passed the spot, then began slowing rapidly.

When they reached a section of pavement that had been milled away, leaving small furrows lengthwise, Ranger cut his speed. It took an expert's touch to just keep them in their lane, but the truck held its course.

They raced around a curve, and by then the fugitive was less than five car lengths ahead. He was wobbling badly back and forth in the center of the highway. Ranger touched the brakes, sensing they were closing in too fast.

"He's either in trouble, or trying to keep us from passing him," she said.

"He's got two wheels on the high side, and two on the low, rough side. That's making it hard for him to keep control of his car," Ranger said. His headlights, the new extra-bright lamps, showed an object farther ahead, just beyond Finch's car.

"Something's on the road—a rock slide," Dana said, leaning forward and gripping the dash.

The small sedan straddled the center line and Finch swerved back to the right, barely missing the loose rocks and debris. Suddenly there was a puff of smoke and pieces of his left rear tire flew back at them.

"Hang on!" Ranger called out. A chunk of rubber struck the windshield with a loud thump, then disappeared over the top of the car.

They zigged and zagged, the truck bouncing and

skidding, but Ranger somehow kept them on the road. Dana's eyes were glued on the car ahead. Then the sedan suddenly tumbled off the road and disappeared from sight.

Ranger slammed on the brakes, coming to a full stop. "Don't move!" He put the truck in Reverse, backed up about fifty yards, then parked.

Ranger switched on the truck's emergency flashers, then handed Dana his cell phone. "Try to get 911. I'm going down there," he said, grabbing a large flashlight.

"I'll follow you. I may be able to help."

Dana contacted the local sheriff's office, then inched down the steep mountain slope, using a smaller flashlight he'd kept on the console. The way was difficult and steep, but she took it slow, tracing Ranger's route.

Finally she reached the car. It was upside down and nearly flat from the beating it had taken coming down the mountain side.

"I don't see him anywhere and the driver's door was ripped off." Ranger shifted the beam to the area around the wreck, then stopped. "Found him."

The light revealed Finch's head, torso and right arm. The rest of his body was pinned beneath the vehicle, which reeked of gasoline.

"He was one of the kidnappers," Dana said, fighting the sick feeling at the pit of her stomach.

"But we can't let him die like this. We've got to get him away from the car before it catches on fire."

Ranger moved in closer, then realized the man was already dead. Though his eyes were open, they registered nothing.

Ranger took a step back as a flash, then sparks, ignited around them. A flame appeared on the ground at the front of the car, then spread upward into the engine compartment in just a few seconds.

"A fire extinguisher. The one in your truck," Dana yelled. Before she'd even finished speaking, there was a loud whoosh and a wave of pure heat slammed against her.

"He's dead," Ranger said, forcing her back. "Move farther away. The gas tank's going to go."

Dana pulled free. "We've got to do *something*."

"He's beyond help, but you're not." He pulled her back hard, away from the inferno. "It's over," Ranger said, wrapping his arms tightly around her.

"Death is all we ever find!" Choking back sobs, Dana buried her head against his shoulder.

He held her tightly while she cried. Minutes passed, but he didn't ease his hold until, exhausted, she stepped away. Before she could go far, he reached for her hand and pulled her back.

Ranger cupped her chin, forcing her to look at him. "We *have* made progress, Dana. We're closing the net around Trujillo," he said, then, in a soft but strong voice, added, "But more than that's happening."

He pointed to the clusters of fading yellow wildflowers still clinging to the hillside. "Open your eyes and you'll see that even in sad times, there's still beauty all around you. Life balances itself out, but you have to be open to the good it brings. If you look for the pattern, you'll see that even evil has a purpose, and good is never far behind."

Ranger bent down slowly and took her mouth in a kiss as gentle as a summer rain. She responded naturally to his tenderness, needing his love more than ever to balance against the violence that surrounded them.

At long last, hearing sirens in the distance, he eased his hold and took her hand. "Let's climb back up to the top. An emergency crew will be here soon, so it's time for us to move along quietly and quickly."

"Like the wind," she said as a cold night breeze swept down the mountain.

"If you're willing to listen, Wind will whisper secrets to you. Wind can be your best friend—or your worst enemy."

She looked down at the hand that held hers. It was exquisitely gentle at times…or deadly. In a soft voice, she answered, "You *are* Wind."

Chapter Twenty

On the way back up to the highway, Ranger called the sheriff's department and gave them a quick rundown of the accident. By the time they reached the road, a Montezuma County sheriff's department vehicle was on the scene.

Ranger recognized the deputy as one of the warriors in the Brotherhood of Warriors, though he didn't know his name. Once he approached, Ranger could read his name tag. "Officer Billie, what can I do for you?"

"Agent Harris of the FBI asked us to send you back to the tribal police station in Shiprock. You're needed there. Follow me."

"No escort's needed. I know the way," Ranger answered.

"Not my call. Agent Harris wants you there, pronto, and I'm going to clear the way for you to the state line. From there, a tribal officer will take over."

As the officer walked back to his vehicle, Dana glanced at Ranger. "That didn't sound good."

"Maybe Harris has news for us," he answered, not really counting on it. He knew Harris. The Bureau man had probably already learned about Finch and the accident, and needed someone to take the heat.

The drive into New Mexico, then back to Shiprock, took less time than the drive up, thanks to the escort and the fact that it was closer to dawn than midnight.

They stepped inside Agent Harris's temporary field office two minutes after arriving at the Shiprock station.

Harris glowered at Ranger. "You didn't give us much lead time, Blueeyes. You trying to jerk me around?"

"Situations change quickly sometimes," Ranger replied in a detached voice. He didn't want to volunteer any information, particularly because of the way he'd learned about Finch's location.

"I've got an update for you," Harris continued. "I've been on the phone for the past half hour, and we managed to squelch the story. No reports of Finch's death will appear in the papers or on TV for now. The deputy he shot has been cleared by the paramedics and is now assisting at the scene. The sheriff is cooperating fully on this, even making up a cover story about the incident at the lodge. I don't want Trujillo to know one of his players is down for the count. We may be able to play this to our advantage."

"Even if the name isn't reported, the accident will raise questions," Dana pointed out.

"*Nothing* will appear in the papers except for a story about somebody stealing and torching a car."

"The FBI can do that?" she asked, surprised.

He looked visibly annoyed. "We're working in conjunction with another local agency that also has an interest in making sure the facts remain hidden for a few days. It's all worked out. Anything else you need explained?"

She glared at him. "No need for sarcasm, Agent Harris."

"You don't *want* to see me with an attitude, Ms. Seles," he growled. "But here's a news flash for both of you," he said steely-eyed. "This is *my* case. If I even dream that either of you is withholding evidence, you'll find yourselves in jail before your next heartbeat. Got it?"

As they walked out, Dana glanced at Ranger, who looked a million miles away. "Squelching that story took more pull than a simple request from a local FBI agent, don't you think?"

"Our medicine man's death sent shock waves across the Navajo Nation. Important people have important friends," he said. Before he could say anything more his cell phone rang. It was Maria Charley.

"Hey, Maria, I almost gave up on you," he said. "You up already, huh?" He looked at his watch and saw it was 5:00 a.m. Ranger put her on the speaker, then held the phone between them so Dana could hear.

"I've got animals to feed and water, remember?" she said. "The good news is that I've got the information you asked me to get you. The brown uniform, remember?"

"What do you have?" Ranger answered.

"Trash collectors wear light brown, and our animal control officers wear a darker brown."

"I need another favor," Ranger said.

"I should have known," Maria said with a belabored sigh. "What is it?"

"Find out if Ignacio Trujillo has dogs and, if so, what address is listed on the animal license."

"That'll take awhile. They don't answer their phones before nine, and I'll have to beg Claire, and send over fry bread or something. Claire responds well to food-type bribes," Maria said. "I'll cover the fry bread, but you'll owe me dinner now."

"Deal."

It was still dark outside, and Dana was struggling to stay awake. Ranger saw her nodding off, then shift and sit up, trying to remain alert. "Feel free to lie back and catch some sleep," he said.

"You've got to be dead tired, too. We both need to rest. Is there a safe place near here we can use to crash for a few hours?"

He thought about it for a moment. The mention of dogs had reminded him of his *Shicheii,* grandfather, who'd loved his companions. "The safest place I can think of is my grandfather's old hogan. He died many years ago overseas. Nobody lives there now, but it's a solid shelter and there's no one around for miles."

"Let's go and, on the way, tell me why you asked Maria that question about the dogs."

"Ignacio's late brother had guard dogs around his place, and my guess is that Ignacio inherited them," he answered. "Licenses are required, and Trujillo isn't going to risk getting in trouble over such a small issue, so he probably did the paperwork. With luck, that'll give us another address to check out."

"If we do manage to track down where Trujillo's hiding out, I've got a plan that may help us get some evidence against him." Seeing his interested look, she continued. "Trujillo's paying his men in cash and that requires him to have large amounts handy. Right now, since he's trying to stay under the radar, he'll be depending on however much cash he has on hand instead of going to the bank. So what we need to do is separate Ignacio from his money. Steal it, or make it impossible somehow for him to get access to that cash."

"That'll be tricky, but I'll sleep on it," he said.

After driving south through Shiprock, he turned down a dirt track, then circled back east, skirting a big arroyo. Finally he parked the truck in front of the only structure visible for miles, an unusual-looking hogan at the base of a hillside.

"Where are we?" she asked, looking around and trying to get a fix on their new location. Dawn was coming soon, giving Dana just enough light to orient herself.

"It feels like we're in the middle of nowhere, doesn't it?" But we're not. There's a trading post a few miles southwest of here, and we're just a mile west of the highway. We made a big circle, nearly."

Ranger took the wool blanket from behind the seat of the pickup, then led the way inside. "My grandfather performed many healing ceremonies here at one time."

"He was a medicine man? A Singer?"

He nodded, looking around, a faraway look on his face. "He was one of our best. I used to sit right there," he said, pointing with his lips, "while he told me the old stories about our gods and how our ceremonies came to be." He paused for a long moment. "When it's quiet, I can almost hear his voice."

"I've never seen a hogan like this, made of poles tied together instead of logs."

He ran his hand over the sturdy wooden posts. "This type of hogan is called the Forked Together House. It's the result of lessons given to us by Talking God, the greatest of all Navajo gods."

Dana looked around. The floor of the hogan had been dug out a foot or more, leaving a bench near the wall that could also serve for storage. Everything had a simple beauty that spoke of decades long past. The blankets on the ground were frayed, but she could see the grandeur they'd once held.

"You or your brother must come out here every once in a while to maintain the place. There are no weeds, leaves, or any sign of four-footed 'visitors'."

"We take turns. I checked the place out last month."

He spread their blanket on the ground, lay down, then stretched out his arms to receive her. "You can rest against me. My shoulder will be your pillow."

"There was a time when I couldn't go to sleep unless I was safe at home," she murmured, settling against him, then drifting off.

"You've found a new one, *sawe,*" he said, using the Navajo word for sweetheart, "in my arms."

DANA SENSED Ranger's absence even before she'd opened her eyes. Sunlight was filtering past the worn blanket that served as a door as she sat up. Realizing she was alone in the cold hogan, fear gripped her.

Then she heard Ranger's rich baritone voice nearby, rising in a haunting chant that spoke of history and the wisdom of the ages. Moving quietly as to not disturb him, she went outside and saw him open his *jish,* take a pinch of pollen out, touch it to the tip of his tongue, then throw it upward toward the heavens.

Although she hadn't made a sound, he'd sensed her presence. "Did I wake you?" he asked, turning to face her.

Only by not being there. But she kept that answer to herself. "That was a beautiful chant," she said.

"It's a *Hozonji,* a song of blessing," he answered, then wanting her to understand him, added, "When you take care of what's most important first, other things eventually fall into place."

Dana nodded in silent agreement. Ranger's strength came from more than his toned body, training and intelligence. His beliefs made him the man he was.

She followed him back inside the hogan and helped him gather their things. "Do you think your friend will get back to us today with the rest of the information we need?"

He nodded. "I'm almost certain of it."

"We should try to eat along the way," she said as they got underway, circling around toward the highway.

"There'll be people selling *naniscaada* sandwiches, made with homemade tortillas or fry bread, out of the back of their trucks between here and Shiprock. That's the best rez food there is."

THEY'D JUST REACHED the highway when his cell phone rang. Glancing at the caller ID, he put the phone on speaker. "Good morning, Maria," he said.

"I have the address. 222 Canyon Way in Bloomfield. When I accessed the address of the registered pet owner, the software also listed a complaint filed just yesterday. Two vicious dogs have allegedly been harassing children through the bars of the front gate. Animal control is scheduled to make a visit this afternoon to check it out."

"That's his main address," Ranger said, surprised. "Trujillo owns several properties and he's been moving around. That's why the FBI hasn't been able to zero in on him. But it sure sounds like he's back there now. Any chance of you asking animal control to hold off on their investigation until tomorrow?"

"Do I want to know why?"

"Not really."

"No surprise. I'll make the request, but no guarantees."

"I understand. And, Maria, thanks again."

"Remember, you owe me."

"I will, and thanks," he said, hanging up and looking over at Dana. "Trujillo will undoubtedly move on after a visit from animal control, so we need to get over there as soon as possible and re-connoiter," Ranger said. "Maybe we can find a way to put your plan in motion."

"Food first," Dana said as her stomach rumbled loudly.

He chuckled. "Good idea. Otherwise, your stomach will give us away for sure."

RANGER LAY FLAT on his stomach, surveying the gated mansion from the adjacent hillside. Two Doberman pinschers had been given free run of the grounds, and they made frequent stops at the gate to sniff and posture. Ranger handed the binoculars to Dana so she could take a look, then called his brother.

Ranger gave Hunter a quick rundown. "I'm planning on taking a clandestine tour. Is there any intel we can get on the house, or maybe on Trujillo's habits? We're looking for a stash of cash he'd keep nearby."

"I can get you the plans to the house in a short time, but as far as his habits…that might take some time."

"That could be a problem. Our man's scheduled for a visit from animal control. Once they come by, he'll probably pick up stakes and move on."

"Hang tight. I'll see what I can do," Hunter answered.

They waited for over thirty minutes and Ranger used the time to maintain surveillance on Trujillo's estate. He needed to get a feel for the place and its rhythms.

When his phone rang, Ranger was ready.

"I've got some intel," Hunter said. "About four months ago, Ignacio accused his housekeeper of stealing and fired her. But as it turns out, her cousin's one of ours. According to what she told him, Ignacio has a safe in each of his homes, every one of them behind paintings above the bedroom dressers."

"Got it. Thanks."

"But she also said that every house is full of alarms."

"I'll be on the lookout."

"We'll set up a watch on the place. That way if he bolts we'll still be right on his tail," Hunter said.

After Ranger hung up, Dana glanced over at him. "We're going to need a really good plan to get into that house. I don't want to be a hot lunch for those guard dogs."

"Don't worry about them. I've got that covered. My *Shicheii* taught me something that'll take care of that problem without harming the animals."

KNOWING THAT GETTING on Trujillo's property would be tricky, Dana had insisted on a diversion. Ranger had heard her out and agreed on her plan.

On schedule, Dana called Agent Harris and let him know where Trujillo was. Then, before he could inundate her with questions, she hung up.

"You were right. He already knew about this place," she told Ranger. "He asked me how we'd found this address even before I'd finished giving it to him. But if Harris was waiting for Trujillo to make a move before closing in on him, we've now forced the agent's hand."

They didn't have to wait long before Agent Harris and two county deputies came to pay Trujillo a visit.

"They're all in the front room," Ranger said, looking through the binoculars. "One of Trujillo's men is watching the front gate, but we can bypass him altogether if we climb the adobe wall out back."

"And lower ourselves into the jaws of his killer dogs…"

"Don't worry. I told you, I've got that covered. Just stay behind me," he said.

"Count on it," she answered with a hesitant smile.

"Our biggest problem once we're inside will be bypassing the alarms. Whatever you do, don't touch anything."

"I've got a good eye for detail. If I spot anything, I'll give you a heads-up. I just wish we weren't doing this in broad daylight."

"That's going to work in our favor. No one will expect a break-in now, especially while the FBI and police are inside. And the fact that someone's at home means the internal motion sensors will probably be turned off."

They stopped by his truck and Ranger picked up a small backpack.

"What's in there?" she asked.

"Everything I might need," he said, slipping it over his shoulder.

They walked down a side road, crossed the street, then stepped over to the six-foot-high adobe wall. Ranger went over first. "Come on," he whispered a few seconds later.

She jumped up, scrambled to the top, then lowered herself quickly to the ground. "The dogs?"

"Don't run, just walk—quickly—to the back of the house."

Before she could take a step, the two guard dogs came running around the corner. Spotting intruders, their hackles rose, and they rushed at them, low to the ground, teeth bared, snarling.

Ranger stood in front of her, reached into his pocket and brought out a small reddish-brown spear point. Not looking at the dogs, he focused on the stone, whispering in Navajo.

Terrified, Dana closed her eyes and pressed her back to the wall. After only a few seconds, she couldn't hear the dogs anymore. Opening one eye, she peered out. To her amazement, both dogs had stopped about four feet away and were now sitting, alert but calm.

Ranger then whispered something else, and both dogs lay down.

"It's like they've been hypnotized. What's in that stone?" she whispered to Ranger.

"It's flint. The way light flashes off it represents lightning and predawn." Without looking back at the dogs, they walked quickly around to the back of the large adobe home. "Flint was created when the hides of the monsters that preyed on the earth disintegrated. It has power and can restore harmony."

When they reached the corner, she glanced back, but the dogs still hadn't moved.

Ranger walked over to the big wooden door, then pointed to a small sensor near the wrought-iron handle. "We've got to disable this before we open the door."

He reached into his backpack, pulled out a

slender piece of magnetized material, then stuck it to the sensor.

No alarms went off when they slipped inside. The house was old, with thick walls, but they could hear Agent Harris a few rooms away, hammering Trujillo with question after question. Trujillo didn't seem overly disturbed, and spoke quietly in response.

Ranger gestured down the long hallway, and Dana followed, trying to move as silently as he did. They reached the master suite several seconds later. This room, with a brick floor, high-beamed ceiling and colorful area rugs, was as big as her entire house. The door was open, but Ranger closed it behind them, turning the small lever that locked it shut.

Ranger pointed to the painting over the dresser, then moved around in front of it, studying the setup. Again, using small magnets to trick the mechanisms into sending a closed circuit signal, he was able to pull back the hinged painting without triggering an alarm. Behind it was a small safe with a door the size of a piece of notebook paper and a dial that reminded Dana of a big combination lock.

Ranger reached down into his backpack again. She half expected him to pull out something high tech, like a laser blowtorch. When he brought out a stethoscope, she chuckled softly.

Seeing her expression, he whispered. "It's a cheap, old design safe. I'll be able to break into it fairly quickly. Go over to the door and listen for anyone coming down the hall."

She stood by the door, listening, but all she could hear was Agent Harris's voice. After a few minutes, she turned to see how Ranger was doing. The safe was already open, and he was setting bundles of cash on the bed. "We're not going to steal it," he whispered. "We're only going to relocate the stuff. How about behind the cold air return vent?" He pointed to a grill just above the baseboard.

"I'll unscrew it for you," she said. "It sounds like Harris is still giving Trujillo some heat."

He handed her a small mechanical screwdriver with several head choices, and while she transferred the money, he took a CD from the safe and put it inside a desk top computer across the room and made a copy. He repeated the process with two more disks, then placed the originals back in the safe and closed it up.

"Why didn't you just take the originals?" she asked.

"I don't want him to cover his tracks. I want him to think that one of his employees or goons was looking for a quick score and took his cash. I bet he's got the combination hidden around here someplace anyway."

As they slipped back out into the hallway, Dana could hear Agent Harris still grilling Trujillo.

Judging from Trujillo's sarcastic responses, she was sure he believed he was untouchable. Maybe the loss of so much cash would get a reaction from the lowlife, and undercut his cocky arrogance. They needed to push him into making a mistake and exposing himself directly.

They stepped outside seconds later and to Dana's surprise the two dogs were still lying down as if on "stay." "Wow," she whispered.

He held one finger over his mouth and hurried across the grounds toward the wall, his hand in hers.

Once they'd gone over the adobe wall, Ranger poked his head over and whistled. The Dobermans jumped up and ran over to the wall, barking furiously.

Dana said nothing until they were in Ranger's truck almost a mile away. "That was really something back there…what you did with the dogs, I mean. You never cease to amaze me. Every time I think I know you, I discover something new."

"Is that a bad thing?"

She smiled slowly and gave him an honest answer. "Not so far."

Chapter Twenty-One

Ranger took her to the one place he'd never thought he'd take anyone outside the brotherhood—the old reconverted barn deep on the reservation where new warriors trained. But he'd known it would be empty inside now. The brotherhood was in a state of transition. No one would be initiated anytime soon.

"What is this place?" she asked at they arrived.

"Kind of a private gym…and, at the moment, our place of refuge," he said. "I needed someplace where I could study these CDs in relative safety." And safe they would be. He'd felt the presence of some of his brother warriors, watching, as they drove up. The fact that they hadn't been intercepted meant that he'd been recognized by at least one pair of eyes.

He led her into a small, unoccupied office that bordered a large arena, and got down to work almost immediately. Dana didn't interrupt him while he loaded the CDs into his laptop and studied what they contained.

"This one looks like an accounts payable ledger, but it doesn't list the last names of the payees—the people he hired," he said at last. "A few months ago he hired someone by the name of Del. No last name, but undoubtedly the dead man's partner," he said, avoiding mentioning Marc Finch by name.

"Scroll down more. There's a lot of information there," she said, standing behind him and studying the entries.

It took them almost twenty minutes, but they finally found a separate accounting base and another entry that dated back ten months. "There you go. Del Archuleta," she read off. "He's a P.I., according to that. Have you ever heard of him?"

"No, but I can have him checked out." Ranger dialed his brother, then waited. "I need some intel," he said, then proceeded to tell him what they'd learned.

Hunter's response was immediate. "I'll get back to you. And Wind…? You'll have to explain your choice of sanctuary to the brotherhood when all this is over."

"Understood," Ranger said and hung up. He'd known he was violating security by coming here with Dana and that would make him subject to disciplinary measures later. But, as always, he'd done what was necessary. "Let's see what else these other accounts have to tell us," he said, focusing back on the screen.

Another half hour passed, but they found nothing else they could use. "At least we have Del's full name," Dana said. "That'll help us narrow the search. I think we've made some solid progress. Maybe I'll be able to meet with *Hastiin Dííl* soon."

Before he could answer, his cell phone rang. He flicked it open and answered.

"Del Archuleta, according to a uniformed agency source, is a scumbag," Hunter said. "He had his P.I. ticket pulled last year for playing both sides of the fence on a divorce case. I've got his last known address and two photos, and I'm uploading them now. Maybe the woman will recognize them."

Ranger switched screens and picked up his e-mail. "Do either of these men look familiar to you?" he asked her.

As she leaned over him to take a closer look at the screen, he grew aware of every part of her. Though she'd given herself to him, it had been on her own terms. Her body had been his, but she'd held back a piece of her heart. That knowledge tugged hard at him. Next time, there would be no holding back, not by her, and not by him, either.

"The one on the left. He was one of the men who kidnapped us," she said, interrupting his thoughts.

He had to struggle to refocus. "And the other one?"

"I haven't seen him before."

Reading his brother's note, Ranger filled her in.

"The one you recognized is Bruce—Del Archuleta's brother. He used to work for the city of Farmington as an animal control officer."

Ranger passed the news to Hunter, then hung up, avoiding what would have undoubtedly been his brother's next question—what was next on their agenda.

"We need to find Bruce and Del, and we have Del's last known address. What do you say we go pay him a visit?" he said.

"I'm ready when you are," she answered.

They drove to the address they had for Del and found he'd moved. The new tenant, a young, slim, college-aged woman, seemed to want Ranger to stick around, so she invited them in.

"I've forwarded a few pieces of mail to Del, and I've got his new address around here someplace," she said, brushing back a strand of long, blond hair. "He lives with his creepy brother, Bruce." She fished around a drawer for a few moments, then finally pulled out a small notepad. "Here it is," she said, handing it to Ranger.

Dana tried not to feel ignored, but the woman hadn't taken her eyes off Ranger since they'd come in.

Ranger gave the young woman one of his devastating smiles. "I appreciate your help."

"Let me know if you need anything else. My

casa is your *casa,* as they say around here." She stepped closer and gazed up at him. "Good luck."

As they drove to the address she'd given them, Dana laughed. "I felt like the invisible woman back there."

"Jealous?" he teased, then shaking his head, added, "Nah, you're way too secure for that."

She thought about what he'd said. "It's a funny thing about security. I spent most of my life trying to create it for myself—through my job, my friends, my lifestyle. But these past few days, as we fought just to stay alive, I learned that security isn't a tangible thing, it's a spiritual outlook. Security comes from courage, and faith, in yourself…and in those you trust."

For the first time Ranger saw hope for them and not just for a few stolen moments here and there.

They reached the address a short time later. Ranger parked about half a block down the street from the small one-story house and waited. "They're both in there, judging by the two cars in the driveway," he said after a moment. "Unless one of them has a visitor."

"No, Bruce is there. I just saw him pass by the window," she said, her voice shaky as she handed him the binoculars. "I'll never forget his face."

"Don't let him get to you," he said. "He's going down."

"I just remember…him. He was one of the men who questioned the medicine man. When I see his face…I see death."

"Stay here," he said. "I'm moving in."

"I'm going with you. There are two of them, and that's not an even playing field. I can help balance the odds a bit."

"All right then. I'll watch your back and you watch mine."

Ranger checked the pistol in his belt, then started the truck and drove down the street. He killed the engine as they got close, and coasted into the driveway silently, blocking both vehicles.

Ranger nodded to Dana, then climbed out of the pickup and walked over to the door. She stood behind him, and to the left as he knocked hard on the door four times. Then he pushed the doorbell, not taking his finger off.

"Del, gotta talk to you, man. Business," he yelled, faking a southern New Mexico accent.

As Del yanked open the door, Bruce reached around Del and slammed the door shut.

"Run!" they heard him yell.

Ranger kicked the door open instantly and the force of it knocked Del to the floor. Ranger was on him in a second. Grabbing him by the back of the collar, he swung Del around, bouncing him off the wall.

"If he tries to get up, shoot him wherever you want," he said, handing Dana a small pistol pulled from his jacket pocket. "And grab that cell phone," he added, pointing to a unit on the coffee table, an idea forming in his mind.

Ranger raced across the living room just as Bruce went out the back door, slamming it shut. By the time Ranger opened it again, the fugitive was already pulling himself up the cinder-block wall across the backyard.

Ranger jumped over the wall, landing in a crouch, his hand on the butt of his pistol. Bruce was nowhere in sight.

Ranger stood still and listened. Hollow footsteps came from his right. Taking three steps, Ranger jumped down into the dry irrigation ditch that bordered the property. Bruce was fifty feet ahead, sprinting around the curve in the dry channel that ran underneath the street about a hundred yards away.

Ranger pressed hard, gaining ground, but Bruce ran up the concrete apron lining the ditch at the bridge. A second later a woman screamed.

Running up the concrete, Ranger reached the street level just as a green pickup raced away, Bruce at the wheel. An elderly Navajo woman lay on her side on the asphalt. As Ranger ran over to help her, the woman rose to her knees, shaking her fist at the departing pickup and cursing colorfully.

Ranger thought of a few more pertinent words to add to the string of obscenities. He'd lost the race, and there was no way he'd catch up to Bruce anytime soon.

Ranger made a quick call to Agent Harris, updating him on all the events. Before Harris could go on a tirade, Ranger abruptly ended the call. There'd be hell to pay later, but for now, he had other business.

After making sure the woman was all right, he returned to Bruce's duplex. Del was sitting on the floor, and Dana still had him at gunpoint.

"Del, you're in one heckuva lot of trouble," Ranger said casually, taking a seat across from him. "I'm going to turn you over to the feds, but I need some fast answers. Cooperate with me, and I'll return the favor when you go before the D.A."

"Forget it. I'm not talking," Del spat out.

"Trujillo's got his own problems right now," Ranger said. "I wouldn't worry about him sending anyone after you." Even as he said the words, he knew that Trujillo probably still had other assets, and with those he'd be able to buy himself a new bunch of men.

Del shook his head. "People like that never forgive or forget."

Ranger considered it for a moment, then took Dana aside. "I'm going to tie Del up and leave him here for Agent Harris. But you and I need to get going."

"What if his brother returns?" Dana countered. "He'll free Del."

"Bruce won't be coming back here. He's probably looking for another vehicle right now."

Ranger took the cell phone from Dana, shoved it in his shirt pocket, then tied Del up to the frame of the sofa with rope taken from the curtain rods. They were out of the house five minutes later. Two blocks from the house several police cruisers, sirens blaring, roared past them.

"What's next?" she asked.

He handed her Del's cell phone. "Does he have Ignacio on speed dial?"

Dana checked it out. "There's an *I.T.* listed so I think that's probably him," she said.

"Okay. Now I'm going to need something my brother has...or, more accurately, the brotherhood does."

This was the first time he'd mentioned the brotherhood by name, and she gave him a surprised look.

He met her gaze, then focused back on the road. "You've risked your life repeatedly to help us. You've earned the right to be trusted," he said.

"Will the others think that, too?" she asked in a soft voice.

"Once they know the whole story, yes," he said slowly. "We can be ruthless with our enemies, but we also know how to honor our friends."

He picked up the phone and called Hunter. "I need a piece of equipment—the voice scrambler gizmo. I have plans for it."

"Okay, but we can't use any of our usual drop sites because we don't know which—if any—have been compromised," he said. "So go to the place where you used to exchange notes with your first girlfriend, the preacher's daughter. Remember?"

"Of course."

"It'll be there in twenty minutes. Give me twenty-five before making the pickup."

"Okay. Thanks," Ranger said, ending the call, then checking his watch.

As Ranger drove, he explained where they were going. "It's a huge elm that died years ago, but there's a knot in the trunk that comes out if you pull, and a space inside for hiding things."

"I'm not sure I'm following you. Why do you need to disguise your voice?"

"Using Del's phone, I'm going to call Trujillo, and let him assume I'm Del. I'll tell him that I've been taking all the risks and I'm sick of the whole thing. I'll threaten to spill my guts to the feds unless I get more up-front money."

"He'll suspect a trap. Trujillo knows Del has as much to lose as he does. And what about Bruce? He could contact Trujillo at any time and blow your plan to shreds. We need a better hook."

They reached the drop site a short time later and, as they got close to the elm, she saw two sets of initials carved into the trunk. "So who is JB?"

He grinned. "I had it bad for Janet Begay back then," he said, working the knot in the center of the trunk loose. "Her father was a preacher, and he didn't allow his daughter to date. She respected that, so, except for trading notes, the only time we had together was at school."

Dana watched him carefully as he extracted a small device, then placed it in his shirt pocket.

"So what does that do?" she asked.

"You can change the pitch of your voice up and down, and other little tricks. I'm going to use it to fade in and out, like a bad connection."

She nodded slowly. "Good. I have a new idea that'll help us get the evidence we need, and using that device will really help," she added. "When you call, pretending to be Del, tell him you've got the list he wants, but you need a quick payoff because you're getting out of the area. Unless he can make it worth your while, the list of brotherhood members will go up for sale to the highest bidder."

Ranger considered her plan and nodded. "I like it."

"I can give you the name of a brotherhood member—one toward the top of the list that the medicine man gave them while drugged," she added. "Trujillo's probably got that name already and it'll add credibility to your story."

"No. We can't jeopardize another brotherhood member without his knowledge and consent. I'll give him my name and my brother's. Neither will come as a surprise to him," he said. "My brother Hunter played a key role in the operation that brought Ernesto down. And by now he knows I've been guarding you."

Ranger hooked up the electronic device to the phone, entered a few code numbers, then made the call to Trujillo, pretending to be Del. After finishing his say, he waited.

There was a lengthy, tense silence before Trujillo spoke. "There's no place a traitor can hide and when they find your body, somebody's going to lose their breakfast."

"I'll be long gone before you ever order the hit," Ranger countered, "and you don't have the stones to come out of your hidey hole and do it yourself." Before Trujillo could speak, Ranger named the price and saw the surprise register on Dana's face.

"Cut the crap, Del. You think I'm falling for this scam?" Trujillo shot back in an ice-cold tone. "That list got burned in the fire."

"Wrong. That's what you get for trusting someone outside your family. I *obtained* it from a guy who held on to it in case he got pulled in by the feds and needed a bargaining chip. But he doesn't have to worry about that anymore," Ranger said in a deadly voice.

"What's with the connection? You still in the mountains?" Trujillo asked.

"Good try, ex-boss. Here's a little incentive. I'll give you two names from the list just to show you I'm sincere—Hunter and Ranger Blueeyes."

There was a pause. "Good choices, but they're just names. Prove you've got the list."

Ranger paused. "You'll see the list when we meet eye-to-eye."

"No deal."

Dana, realizing that Ranger was losing ground, waved her hand in front of his face, getting his attention, then pointed to herself.

He shook his head, knowing what she was thinking.

"Let me go," she yelled suddenly.

"What's going on?" Trujillo asked immediately.

"TV's on," Ranger shot back, glowering at Dana and moving away from her quickly.

"They'll catch you," Dana yelled out, then cried out as if he'd hit her.

Ranger closed his eyes, then opened them again. There was no turning back now.

"You've got the Seles woman. *That's* where you

got the list," Trujillo said flatly. "Where's Blue-eyes…if he's dead, why haven't I heard about it?"

"Your network's gone, and I'm not admitting anything over a phone. But enough with the questions. You want the list or not?"

"Bring her—and the list of names—and I'll have your money in cash."

"Here's where we'll meet," Ranger said, then gave him a location near the Brotherhood of Warriors' operational base. He and his brothers knew that section of the rez like the palms of their hands.

After Ranger hung up, he glared at Dana. "Have you lost your mind?"

"You were losing him, and I was going to go with you anyway. What's the difference?"

"News flash—you weren't going. Correction, you *aren't* going. There are others I can trust to protect you now."

"In your dreams. Think about it a second. The only way to make sure he goes to prison is if I go along. Selling him the list doesn't mean a thing to the courts, but kidnapping, or attempted murder, will."

"The knowledge of the list and what it represents would have implicated him, Dana. Keep in mind that Glint was *hired* to get that list, and he knew what it was going to be used for. Once Trujillo's in custody, Glint will sing his lungs out."

"Sorry to break it to you, but I would have

come—one way or another. I *need* to see this through, too. And at least this way you'll know where I am."

"There's a comforting thought," he snapped.

"So now we need to arrange the details of this meet," she said. "This is your area of expertise. How do we handle this?"

"With help," he said as he reached for his phone and punched out his brother's number.

"She did *what?*" came Hunter's response less than a minute later.

Ranger glared at her. "It's too late to change anything now. We're going to need some heavy duty backup because I can't guarantee he doesn't suspect a trap. The only thing I'm sure about is that he'll come. He'll risk anything to get his hands on Dana."

Chapter Twenty-Two

The meeting place was to be a site in the desert northeast of the community of Shiprock, just inside reservation land. The bullet-resistant vest she now wore under the heavy jacket was bulky and uncomfortable, not reassuring.

"Nothing's ever fool-proof in an operation like this. Just remember, all Trujillo has to do is see you," Ranger said. "Thanks to the unofficial loan, you've got some protection from handguns and shotguns. But remember to stay inside the truck, and if there's shooting, get down and stay down. The truck's side door panels are reinforced."

They left the highway north of town and headed east along the desert floor. There were oil and gas wells in the area, which meant there were graveled access roads between sites. Their plan was to meet Trujillo at the base of Monument Rocks, the largest formation for miles, just above and west of Eagle Nest Arroyo. From there, no one could get behind them, since the cliff face was directly to their backs. Ranger knew his brother and other brotherhood warriors were already set up in strategic locations, including the arroyo itself. Ranger got out of the truck, and came around to Dana's side.

She'd been watching for the past ten minutes, but the only things she could see in the immediate vicinity were grass, brush, rocks and the edge of the arroyo. "Are you sure we'll have backup? I didn't even see any tire tracks. Maybe we *should* have called Agent Harris."

"He'll have his shot at Trujillo—afterward. There'll be two cameras, directional microphones and several of our people listening in when Trujillo arrives. This is serious tribal business. The FBI may have jurisdiction here, but this is *our* land and *our* fight."

Ranger saw the flash of a mirror off the windshield and tensed up. "It's time. Trujillo's on his way. That was my brother's signal."

Seconds later, a large black SUV came into view in the distance. "One vehicle. Looks like he didn't bring backup," Dana said.

"A big vehicle like that could hold a baseball team *and* their gear. Trujillo didn't come alone. Count on it."

Trujillo was driving, and though he was the only person visible, all the windows were down.

When he arrived he parked to the left of Ranger's truck. Seconds later, Trujillo opened his door and climbed out, his vehicle providing him with partial concealment.

Ranger stepped toward the front of the SUV, wanting to have the cover of the engine in case Trujillo came around with a gun in hand.

Suddenly someone stood up in the SUV, poking his head and arm out of the sunroof. It was Bruce. Ranger ducked below the hood just as Bruce opened fire. The bullets blew away the hood ornament with a loud whine.

Ranger dove to the ground and rolled to his left, wanting to keep Bruce guessing. As he looked underneath, he realized that Trujillo must have jumped back into the SUV.

"Go!" Trujillo yelled.

The doors on the passenger side suddenly flew open, and Bruce and another man leaped out, firing shots at Ranger with pistols as they ran. Bullets kicked up the dust, but Ranger had already disappeared beneath the SUV.

While one man crouched, trying to see where Ranger had gone, Bruce jumped up on the running board of Ranger's pickup. He grabbed Dana through the window with his right hand, his pistol now transferred to his left.

Ranger, on the wrong side of Trujillo's vehicle

to intervene, made the next best move. He jumped onto the running board, grabbed Trujillo's pistol hand and yanked him out the window onto the ground. Trujillo rolled up to his feet, pulled a knife out of a boot sheath, then took one step forward. Suddenly a hail of bullets struck the ground by his feet.

"Don't move!" came a shout from above. Trujillo turned his head and stared at Hunter, who was thirty feet up the side of the cliff, aiming a carbine at his head.

"Don't shoot!" Trujillo yelled back, letting the knife fall as he raised his hands over his head.

Dana pulled away from Bruce's grip, but only to build momentum. She slammed the door with her shoulder as she lifted the handle, whacking Bruce in the face with the side of the door. The blow knocked him to the ground and he dropped his pistol.

Ranger raced around the back of the SUV, surprising the third man, who was aiming his weapon at Dana. He kicked the man in the ribs, then moved in as the guy scrambled back up to his feet. Ranger landed a solid uppercut, and his opponent went down hard.

Ranger looked back at Dana and saw her scooping up Bruce's pistol. Archuleta was flat on his back, holding his bloody face with both hands, moaning.

"Good work," Ranger said, noticing two

warriors running up from the direction of the arroyo, weapons directed at the men on the ground.

Two more armed warriors, who'd come out of the arroyo in another spot, were already approaching Trujillo. Their captive was cursing, but standing dead still, his arms in the air, as Hunter kept him in his sights.

By the time Ranger walked back between the vehicles, Dana was sitting on the running board of his truck. The pistol was still in her hand, but pointing down to the ground.

He'd just joined her when his phone rang and he heard Hunter's voice. "I didn't want to have this conversation in front of Trujillo and his men. The tribal police and Agent Harris are on their way. We'll be handing these punks over to them as soon as they get here. We also have some great video and audio waiting for them. Once you give Harris your statements and can leave the scene, come to the cave of secrets. *Hastiin Díil* wants to meet with Ms. Seles."

TRUJILLO AND HIS GANG were loaded into patrol units and taken away, and after answering Agent Harris's barrage of questions, Dana and Ranger were finally free to leave.

Dana walked with Ranger back to his truck. "This part's done, and everyone's safe now, but I've still got a promise to keep."

"*Hastiin Dííl*'s ready to meet with you," he said. "I've been ordered to take you to a place no outsider has ever been—the heart of the Brotherhood of Warriors. This is unprecedented. But first, on behalf of the brotherhood, I need your word that you'll never reveal its location, or anything else about your visit."

"You have it," she said, a shiver of excitement racing up her spine. "The secret will be safe with me."

"I believe you," he answered quietly. Her unshakable loyalty was what made her the woman who'd touched his heart…and now held it in the palm of her hand.

"But does *Hastiin Dííl* even need the list anymore?" she asked. "He must have managed to get the names he needed, or we wouldn't have had any help when we confronted Trujillo."

"*Some* of our warriors were there, but not all. Our secondary identification process is…lengthy."

The drive took almost two hours, but finally they reached the foothills east of Gallup, near the southern tip of the Navajo Nation.

"This is it," he said at last, parking beneath a tall piñon pine. They were in a dry forest of junipers and pines, where the mesas rose almost like stair steps into the high mountains beyond.

"The climb up isn't a difficult one, so don't

worry," he said, seeing her staring at the jagged sandstone cliff, a worried frown on her face.

A sturdy wooden ladder had been set in place for them and Ranger went up first. Dana followed and a few minutes later entered the opening of a deep, narrow cave carved by wind and water into the cliff side. A piñon log fire was burning in a shallow pit surrounded by stones, and the blue sky was visible through the vertical slit above them where the smoke rose and escaped.

Ranger greeted his brother, their fists meeting in the air, then introduced Dana to him.

Dana watched the two brothers, noting how similar their expressions were. Before she could even try to get to know Hunter a bit more, she was led into one of the antechambers. Hunter asked her to wait, then he and Ranger stepped into an adjoining area, leaving her alone.

After they'd left, an elderly man appeared, wearing the white sash of a medicine man. "Welcome to the cave of secrets, schoolteacher. I'm *Hastiin Dííl*." He motioned for her to sit on one of two folded blankets then took a place across from her. "I understand you have a message for me."

The whole story came tumbling out of her and, lastly, she revealed the names, one by one, giving him time to write each down on a piece of hide. "There were more, but I never saw the other part of the list. Before we could do anything about that...we ran out of time," she finished with a whisper. The memory brought tears to her eyes, tears she didn't try to hide or wipe away.

"The brotherhood owes you a great debt." He rolled up the hide, then placed it into a shirt pocket beneath his jacket. "Tell me, what can we do for you? There has to be balance between us."

"I've learned a lot during this journey—about myself and others, too. That knowledge more than cancels out any debt."

He smiled and gave her an approving nod. "One thing remains, then." He called for the others to join them.

Ranger came in first, carrying something in a small box, and handed it to *Hastiin Dííl.*

The medicine man brought out a silver necklace and slipped the chain over Dana's head. "The circle of flames engraved in the medallion is our symbol. This will show that you're under our protection."

Dana thanked him, then met Ranger's gaze and smiled. In this one way she'd be a part of his world forever.

The ceremony concluded, a celebration began. While the food was brought out, Ranger took her hand and pulled her into one of the dark, narrow chambers with him.

"We're bound, you and I," he whispered. "I can't

imagine my life without you in it. I love you, and I'd like to spend my life showing you just how much."

"Starting now?" Welcoming the winds of change, she stepped into his arms.

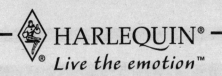

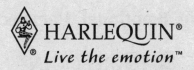

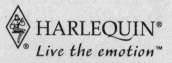

HARLEQUIN®
Presents

The world's bestselling romance series...
The series that brings you your favorite authors,
month after month:

Helen Bianchin...Emma Darcy
Lynne Graham...Penny Jordan
Miranda Lee...Sandra Marton
Anne Mather...Carole Mortimer
Susan Napier...Michelle Reid

and many more uniquely talented authors!

Wealthy, powerful, gorgeous men...
Women who have feelings just like your own...
The stories you love, set in exotic, glamorous locations...

HARLEQUIN®
Presents

Seduction and Passion Guaranteed!

HPDIR104

Harlequin® Historical
Historical Romantic Adventure!

*Imagine a time of chivalrous
knights and unconventional ladies,
roguish rakes and impetuous
heiresses, rugged cowboys
and spirited frontierswomen—
these rich and vivid tales will
capture your imagination!*

*Harlequin Historical...
they're too good to miss!*

HHDIR06

Silhouette®

SPECIAL EDITION™

Emotional, compelling stories that capture the intensity of living, loving and creating a family in today's world.

Silhouette®

Desire

Modern, passionate reads that are powerful and provocative.

Silhouette®

n o c t u r n e

Dramatic and sensual tales of paranormal romance.

Silhouette® Romantic SUSPENSE

Romances that are sparked by danger and fueled by passion.

SDIR07

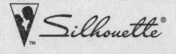